Savannah Joy

By
Winnie Walsh

PublishAmerica
Baltimore

© 2007 by Winnie Walsh.
All rights reserved. No part of this book may be reproduced, stored in a retrieval system or transmitted in any form or by any means without the prior written permission of the publishers, except by a reviewer who may quote brief passages in a review to be printed in a newspaper, magazine or journal.

First printing

All characters appearing in this work are fictitious. Any resemblance to real persons, living or dead, is purely coincidental.

ISBN: 1-4241-6967-4
PUBLISHED BY PUBLISHAMERICA, LLLP
www.publishamerica.com
Baltimore

Printed in the United States of America

To Mary

Chapter 1

Surprised at not having seen her cousin for over twenty years, Marion blurted out, "Elizabeth, is that you? How are you?" Elizabeth, just as stunned, strained to hold on to the leashes holding her two bull dogs, all the while trying to balance a cup of coffee.

"I'll have to continue this conversation another time; these two seem to have the upper hand right now."

"Stop in at the store, we'll have lunch and catch up!" Marion shouted as Elizabeth disappeared around the corner, spilling some of her coffee onto the pavement.

"Catch up my eye," muttered Elizabeth, seething with envy because just before the surprise meeting she noticed Marion's new book, *Women on the Move*, in Shaver's bookstore. *Not only has she a partnership in my father's business, she is getting a name for herself in the literary world.* Elizabeth followed the pull of the two dogs to Lafayette Square, glad she didn't have to engage in any more conversation with her cousin.

After graduation from college in 1984, Elizabeth landed a spot on a local TV station in Savannah, announcing the weather. Within a year other women applied for broadcasting positions and some started anchoring the nightly news. Elizabeth took umbrage at the fact she wasn't considered for any of these spots and complained to management. She believed that the producer of the station showed favoritism toward black women. Both of her parents, Benjamin and Sarah, tried in vain to convince her this wasn't the case. It was difficult to point out to one's own daughter that attitude and personality played an important part in the decision making process. Elizabeth believed she would just bide her time at the TV station and, after some years, head for New York.

Watching a Barbara Walters interview in 1982 with Jimmy Carter, made such an impression on her that she decided broadcast journalism would be her career. However, this came at a difficult time. After her mother's death, Elizabeth announced to her father she received an opportunity to work for NBC in New York. Benjamin thought the antique buying trips his wife, Sarah, had taken Elizabeth on would take her mind off a TV career. She could sniff out excellent pieces at buying shows and successfully bid on them. Her mother said she was a natural and Benjamin thought she would grow to love the business that had been in the family for generations. He took his daughter's decision personally. If it hadn't been for his niece's help at the store after his wife died, he felt the Adams Antique business would have suffered tremendously.

Marion volunteered to help her uncle at the store as much as she could because he seemed overwhelmed at the amount of work he had since his wife's sudden death and the departure of Elizabeth. The volunteer work soon turned into a career for Marion. She enjoyed it and with the death of her husband, Lance, her uncle offered her a partnership in the business to help raise her two children, Stephen and Colleen. His agreement also helped her write; something she did while Lance was alive.

Marion reached the service station, thinking about Elizabeth's contentious departure from Savannah. "Got your car already to go; it needed a new fuel pump." The attendant's high pitch voice interrupted Marion's thoughts of long ago.

"Thank you. Would you mind adjusting the driver's seat? The last time I pulled away I found myself searching for the gas pedal."

"Not a problem." The lanky young man stooped down and reached into the car. "Always forget to do that; thanks for reminding me." Marion paid the bill, got into her car and drove home. She parked her car in front of her house and walked the few steps to her front door. There was a note pinned on it. She pulled the paper away and noticed the store's logo. The note said to meet her uncle at Six Pence the next day at noon. He had something important to discuss with her. *H'mm, wonder if it's about the return of the prodigal daughter.*

Elizabeth finished walking her two dogs and headed for the apartment she rented on East Jones Street. As a young girl, she always liked to stroll down the tree lined street. Her parents lived over the antique store on Bull Street and she never liked the street noise from below. One could always hear the din of traffic and the voices of people leaving the nearby shops and restaurants. Her arrival in Savannah surprised not only her cousin but her dad as well. She just appeared at the store soon after settling in her apartment.

"Hello, Dad." Her father was lifting a crate onto the counter top and his back was to the door. The surprise greeting caused him to drop the crate before he was able to place it on top. "I'm sorry, Dad; I didn't mean to startle you. Here, let me help you."

"That's OK. I've got it now. When did you get into town?"

"A few days ago. Where's Marion? I thought she worked here."

"She does but she's out of town on a buying trip. Why didn't you let me know you were coming home? Did you lose your job in New York? How long are you staying?"

"Whoa, hold up on the questions. One at a time. The answer to the first is I wanted to surprise you, to the second is no, and the third I'm on assignment to do an article on Savannah."

"What kind of assignment? I would think everything there is to know about our town has been already recorded in books and movies by now," he said while reaching for the scissors to tear open the carton. "Why would New York be interested in what goes on down here?"

"There was a rumor going around at a Christi's auction that a Revolutionary artifact of great importance had been discovered here in Savannah. I must have mentioned I was raised here in the antique business."

"I haven't heard any such type rumor and if I did I certainly wouldn't want any big network from New York snooping around. If there was such an article, the owner would soon price it out of a dealer's range."

"I can see why you wouldn't but that's the job I was sent down to do. I guess that leaves you out of any help if you do hear of anything." Benjamin held back the anger he felt for his daughter. *What nerve, coming back after all these years and asking me for help. Where were you when your mother died? If it wasn't for Marion's help, I don't know what I would have done.*

"You're right, I wouldn't." Elizabeth felt the coldness in his voice and decided to end the unexpected visit. *He's never forgiven me after all these years.*

"I guess I'll try and get settled in my apartment."

"Where's that?"

"Jones Street. I always liked it and I found an apartment on the Internet. Suits me fine and they allowed my two dogs. It wasn't easy getting a landlord that would accept animals, but I offered him more than the going rate since my firm will pick up the tab."

"Seems like you did all right for yourself. Well I have to get back to work. I have some cataloging to do and I wanted to finish before Marion gets back."

"She is back. I ran into her on Bull Street. She was surprised to see me too. I didn't get a chance to tell her all that I just told you. We met briefly. It looks like she was headed toward Drayton."

"She mentioned when she called from New York that her car was giving her trouble. I suppose she was headed for the Texaco station to have it fixed when she got home. Glad she made it back. There were some 17th Century Colonial Chairs being auctioned off in New York and she drove up and paid a visit to Stephen at Georgetown on the way up."

"She really has gotten involved in the bidding part of the business." Elizabeth couldn't help but feel jealous of the concern her father had for her cousin. But then there was always favoritism shown Marion even when they were children growing up.

"Look at Marion's essay in the *Savannah Morning News*. It won first place in the essay contest about the Revolutionary War." While Sarah extolled accolades on her niece, Marion walked into the store. Her uncle Benjamin joined in the praise but neither parent noticed the scowl on their daughter Elizabeth's face as she turned and retreated to the back of the store. Benjamin hugged his niece.

"This calls for a celebration, don't you think, Sarah? Don't you think so, Elizabeth?" By now Elizabeth was in her room ripping up her essay and crying. *Marion this, Marion that. One would think she was their daughter. Well, she's not. I am and somehow I'm going to show them. I'll show them all.*

Benjamin shared ownership of the antique business with his sister, Anne, but when she married she sold out to him. Anne married Dan Tobin and they lived out on Wilmington Island with their daughter, Marion. Elizabeth and Marion grew up together and had gone to the same schools. Early on, there seemed to be competition between the girls. At first their parents thought it just sibling rivalry, but as the girls developed into their teens Elizabeth's behavior concerned her mother Sarah. Little things like the essay competition had Sarah wondering just how jealous her daughter was of Marion. Many times Elizabeth complained to her mother about living above the store on Bull Street. Why couldn't they live in a house like her cousin? Both parents tried to explain the necessity of living where they did in case of any fire or water damage that would affect the business. Costly antiques were in the store and if there were any such danger to them they wanted to be near. No amount of cajoling by either parent made a difference. The discussion always ended with Elizabeth storming off to her bedroom and flinging herself on the bed sobbing.

Marion turned the key in the lock, all the while wondering why her uncle had left a note on the door. *Why didn't he leave a message on my voice mail?* The mail lay scattered all over her living room floor. She picked up the pieces, noticing a card from Colleen in Paris. How happy she must be studying at the Sorbonne.

The card said she had been to Versailles and it was glorious seeing the beautiful gardens and learning so much about the French. Marion rifled quickly through the mail. Not much else, she thought and placed it alongside the telephone. She dialed her voice mail and quickly pulled the phone away from her ear. *What in heaven's name is wrong with the phone? Now I know why Uncle Benjamin did what he did.* She then picked up to see if she could dial out. *Good, at least I can dial out.*

"Hello, it's Marion; hope you didn't get the horrible squealing noise on my voice mail, Uncle Benjamin."

"Oh, Marion, it's you; no I just couldn't get into it at all."

"I'll call the phone company right away and see if it's their problem or my answering device."

"Good idea. I guess you know Elizabeth is in town. She mentioned she ran into you the other day. More important, how did the auction go?"

"Very well. I was able to outbid that horrible old Larson and Company for the two chairs. They are gorgeous. I almost would like to keep them myself."

"Now, now, Marion don't get carried away. You sound like your Aunt Sarah. I remember saying to her if we did that too often we wouldn't be in business very long.

"I suppose you're right. I wouldn't have any room in my apartment for them and I don't want to move. Besides, I must draw the line somewhere."

"Elizabeth didn't get a chance to tell you why she is here." Her uncle went on to explain the surprise visit at the store.

"That sounds like exciting news, don't you think so?"

"It does but I didn't let on to Elizabeth that it would be a great find."

"I can imagine. Do you have any money figures?"

"Well after she left I found some catalogues that price artifacts from revolutionary years, and from what I gathered, aside from the historical landmarks, such an item would bring close to a million dollars."

"You're kidding," exclaimed Marion. "Wow, wouldn't that be something. We best start our detective work."

"I'm way ahead of you. I've called city hall and made an appointment with the Restoration committee to see if we can get a list of renovations made in the last ten years. It will be well worth the search, and I'm sure with Elizabeth's knowledge of how to go about tracing something like this we better get started. Once she turns over the information to her employer it becomes public and then all hell will break loose down here. We will have people from all over swarming around here like bees."

Chapter 2

Colleen Tobin strolled down Rue du Madeline, inhaling the smells of flowers in the various stalls, listening to the voices of people conversing in French, observing patrons at café tables reading books and periodicals, all the while savoring their café au lait. This had always been a dream of hers since high school and steered her into the study of the French language. Ever since she had seen the movie *Moulin Rouge*, she wanted to study art and hoped it would be in France. She pulled her down jacket around her, zipping it up because it started to get a little chilly. She had just come back from Versailles where one of her art classes had been held. The trip had been exhilarating and, along with art classes, she enjoyed lectures about Lafayette. There was so much about him she discovered while at these lectures, his involvement with our Revolutionary War, the money he donated to its cause and not accepting pay for his service while serving under Washington. One interesting fact stood out.

The United States Congress of 1778 commissioned Benjamin Franklin to present a gift to him. Franklin had the "best artist in Paris" design an ornamental sword that had a gold handle with engraved scenes from four of the battles in which he had participated in America, along with carved mottoes and coats of arms. Upon his return to France in 1779, this sword was to be presented to him at Versailles by the American representative for all of his generosity in the American Revolution.

During the lecture the professor digressed a bit and added a footnote. The Marquis posed with the sword in a portrait painting that year but the sword had never been seen again after 1780. Some people suspect he lost it when he returned to the colonies in 1780 for the last campaign of the war. Others surmised Benedict Arnold stole it when he escaped to England after committing treason. Colleen loved these little tidbits of mystique.

She was glad she had sent a postcard to her mother from Versailles. Colleen realized how her mother saved for both Stephen and her education…sending the postcard allowed her mother to share her happiness.

"Bon jour," one of her classmates called to her from a sidewalk café. Colleen smiled at the American accent on the French greeting.

"Comment ce va?" Colleen's response drew a blank expression on her classmate's greeting.

"Please sit and translate," moving the opposite chair away from the table with her foot.

"How are you? That's what it means. I only answered in French because you called to me in French.

"Are you kidding? All I remember is the Hail Mary…every morning, Je vous salus Marie, etc. I had a Catholic French teaching order in grammar school and after graduation argued with my parents that I was going to a public high school." Colleen laughed. Louise came from Boston. They talked about classes, professors and the general mayhem that goes with the advent of a new semester. After finishing their drinks the girls left laughing with Colleen trying to teach her friend some French.

The girls arrived back at the dorm and Colleen invited Louise back to her room. Louise helped herself to coffee set up in the room and collapsed onto a bean bag chair. Louise filled Colleen in about life in Boston.

"I made a deal with my parents. I would pay more attention in class if they would give me individual art lessons and so my career in art started, how about you?"

"My dad passed away when I was four, so it's just me, my mom and Stephen, my brother. Stephen is in Georgetown in his last year. My mom works in the antique business in Savannah with her uncle. He's been like a father to both me and my brother ever since my father died. My mother writes as well and has had a few books published."

"That's great; you must tell me the titles and I'll buy the books."

"I'm sure she would like that. Having a request from this side of the Atlantic might just start some interest in Europe." Colleen laughed. "Every little sale helps," she added as she went to her computer and turned it on. "Let's see if there is any mail from home. Great, a letter from Stephen, it's about time he answered my last letter."

"I'll let you catch up on your mail and thanks for volunteering some time to help me catch up on my French. I'll see you in class. Adieu." Louise threw the paper cup in the trash and left.

Dear Colleen,

Sorry it has taken so long to answer you but getting organized at the beginning of a school year can be a busy time as you may well know. So how's the art world going?

Bet you love it. Mom stopped by on her way to New York on a buying trip. We had a great time. She only could stay a day and it so happened it was a Sunday so we did the tourist route and she was surprised at all the security in Washington. But then I told her ever since 9/11 it really has gotten tighter. Even so we did get into many of the buildings after waiting in line for umpteen hours.

I asked her if she would go and check on Beaumont up at Rincon. When I left for school, there was talk about some developer trying to buy up the property and putting up condominiums given its nearness to Mulberry Grove. I hope it never happens because he will have to board elsewhere. Whenever I get a chance to go home I drive out and ride for a day. Even Mom likes to on occasion. Oh well, c'est la vie as you French would say.

Colleen read on with his inquiry on friends, food and classes. She started to type a reply and told about her recent trip to Versailles and meeting her first new friend, Louise.

Chapter 2A

Marion gazed out at the pumpkins spilling over in the fields as she passed them by on her way to Rincon, and wondered if Benjamin had a chance to get a list of the restored houses. *I'm sure Elizabeth has been down to city hall and had a list by now.*

Wish I hadn't promised Stephen to make this trip, but he doesn't ask me for very much. Normally, it was an enjoyable ride because she liked ridding Beaumont once she got there. This time, however, she was not going to saddle up, but rather inquire about all the rumors going around about a developer building condominiums. She couldn't wait to get back to Savannah and start on the research to find some clues as to what artifact, if any, was discovered.

Marion drove up the long driveway to the Butler ranch and noticed Mr. Butler in one of the pastures with his young daughter, Cindy. Stephen started her on riding lessons this past summer and she was doing very well when he left for school. Her father continued the lessons and Marion noticed she had indeed become quite a little horsewoman.

14

"Hello," she called from the car as she alighted and walked toward the two of them.

"Hello yourself," he hollered back over the noise of the mowing going on further down the pasture. He lifted Cindy from the saddle and she raced back to her house.

"She sure is in an awful hurry," turning her head to follow the child's flight.

"Her mother told her they would bake Halloween cookies as soon as she finished her lesson. Are you going to saddle up and ride out for a spell?"

"Not today, I have some business to attend to back in Savannah, but I did promise Stephen I would come out and check on Beaumont. How is he? I suppose he misses Stephen and all his attention."

"I suppose he does but we have one of the hands walk him every day and occasionally someone saddles him up and takes him out. I try and do it every so often once I get caught up."

"I'm sure Stephen appreciates your effort. Oh by the way, there was another motive for the trip. Stephen told me when I visited with him last week he had heard that a developer was out this way looking at property. Is there any chance you would be entertaining selling the ranch?"

"Not a chance. But he was right. A Mr. Bell from Southwest Realtors was out here in late August. He asked Carolyn and me if we would be interested in selling.

"We asked him what his company had in mind. He said he wasn't too sure but they were thinking condominiums. After he left we called some other neighbors, and they too said they had been approached. One of them told us he heard from Council members in Port Wentworth that the Georgia Port Authority was entertaining selling Mulberry Grove to the town so a plantation could be replicated like the one Nathaniel Greene lived in after the Revolutionary War. I suppose with something like that in the area there would be quite a bit of tourism. Who knows? But many of the folks I spoke to said they were just going to sit tight."

"Glad to hear it, and I know Stephen will be too."

"Why don't you come in for a cup of coffee. Carolyn will be disappointed if you don't. She will love to hear how Stephen is doing and maybe you will luck out and enjoy some homemade Halloween cookies."

"Maybe I will; just a quick cup and then I really have to get going."

Chapter 3

"I'm tired of waiting to collect on this," Charles Pickett snarled at antique dealer Art Larson. "It's been three years since I gave you that sword I found at Mulberry Grove. Maybe I should have brought it to some other dealer."

"You mean the sword you stole out of property owned by the Georgia Port Authority. We both know there isn't another antique dealer who would have touched it with a ten foot pole."

In 1975 The Georgia Port Authority bought Mulberry Grove, some of which is listed on The National Register of Historic Places. Charlie Pickett, a petty thief who sometimes came upon an item of historical value not in a very honest way, had struck upon alliance with Art Larson who would fence the item and pay him a nominal fee. Art Larson poured himself a drink. "Patience, Charles, you must have patience. I have to get a release from the original owner before I can put such an item out on the open market. I have my company out there searching."

SAVANNAH JOY

"Who are you kidding? I've seen you get rid of hot stuff before and it never took three years."

"Well this is an entirely different situation. It's too complicated for me to explain the procedure. I must show ownership or the transfer of ownership. Believe me it will be worth your while, you'll see." Charlie grumbled at the last remark, turned and walked toward the door, slamming it behind him as he exited.

Art Larson sat back in his leather easy chair and swirled the brandy in his glass. *If that fool ever realized the find he made, he would have taken it to the Georgia Port Authority. They would have given him more than I would.* Tracing down real ownership had been difficult. The inscription on the sword In Honour of Lafayette indicated the sword belonged to Lafayette but what was it doing in Savannah, Georgia? The people who were tracing it kept running into dead ends. The case it was found in presented a problem as well. The case was similar to one made by blacksmiths in the American Revolutionary War, and this particular case carried an insignia almost like one would see branded on cattle. The mark was that of a horseshoe branded in the leather both inside and out of the case. Charlie said he came upon it by chance when he was out at Mulberry Grove one night looking for anything he could peddle as antiques from the ruins of Nathaniel Greene's plantation that was burned down during the Civil War. He found this sword not too far from the ruins of the General's home. He discovered it while digging around the ruins of a blacksmith's forge. Charlie said it was buried deep under the brick. Art Larson knew he had to sort out all of this, but he had no intention of sharing this information with Charlie.

The fire had been roaring in the fireplace, all the while Charlie had paced back and forth in his tirade about the fee for the artifact. When he left, Art felt a chill and noticed the fire had died down a bit so he rose and walked over to the log holder to place a log on the dwindling flames and reached for the decanter to pour another drink.

"This is a comfortable looking scene," a familiar voice said as he turned to see his son, Tom, standing in the doorway.

"I didn't hear you come in; have a drink. I was just going to pour one for myself."

"Thanks, think I will. It's getting kind of cold outside." Tom approached his father and slouched down into an easy chair beside the fireplace.

"How was the buying trip in New York? Any luck?" Art Larson handed his son the drink.

"Bought a Louis XVI 17th century secretary, but I did want two chairs that Adams outbid me on. Old Benjamin taught Marion a thing or two on bidding maneuvers."

"Yeah, that old goat has been a thorn in my side for years. I thought when his wife died and Elizabeth headed for New York, he would have sold the business. Whoever thought Marion would turn out to be the excellent buyer she is. Oh well, it wasn't a total loss; here, let me get you another drink."

"No thanks, I just wanted to stop and tell you about the Louis XVI." He rose, put down the glass and headed for the door. When his father mentioned Elizabeth's name, he recalled an ugly scene between himself and her many years ago. He just wanted to leave. Elizabeth confided in him at her mother's wake that she had an offer of a job in New York. Tom thought it was insensitive to leave her father so soon after her mother's death, being it was so sudden. They had been seeing each other for sometime and, although they weren't engaged, he was considering asking her to marry him. This news took him by surprise because she never mentioned sending résumés up north looking for jobs.

"How can you just pick up and leave at this time?" He remembered the scene as he headed for his car outside his father's house.

"If I don't accept this offer now, who knows how long I will have to wait before another one comes along." Her voice never wavered as she spoke.

"What about us? Are you just going to leave and expect me to traipse after you when I am committed to business here?"

"You could start an antique business up in New York. You know enough about it. It's not like you would have to change your life. I want something more than a few minutes on the weather. This is a great opportunity for me and I'm not about to pass it up."

"Have you told your father yet?"

"No, but I will. I'm sure he will understand. Maybe Marion can help him out until he gets over my Mom's death. All I know is I am going. My mind is made up." The door of his car scratched the pavement as it swung open. Elizabeth's words, "my mind is made up," played over and over in his head.

Chapter 4

The two children covered themselves with hay and made sure no one saw them get into Lazarus' wagon. They had heard that the Marquis would be in Savannah for three days and wanted to see the famous man Lazarus had served with during the war. While he hammered for hours at his forge, Lazarus would talk about the things this man did in the war against the British.

"An he weren't even an American, he jus' wanted to help fight them Redcoats and have them leave us be. I seen him git off a his horse and fight along the rag and tattered they called an army. I seen him git shot and go right on fighting and firing his musket until he drops to the ground. I remember his men carrying him off to safety and put him a in cart."

"If he wasnna any American what he be?" Leroy the younger of the two asked.

"He be a Frenchman, yessa that's what he be. A rich Frenchman who done left his wife and home to help the cause. And he done come back for the dedication of the monument to Nathaniel Greene in Savannah. Now go on, you two, and be about your own business. If master find you lollygagging around here we both be in trouble. Go on now, be about your work."

Lazarus had asked permission from his employer to go into Savannah to see the dedication of the monument and the two children. Leroy and Samuel knew about it. Nathaniel Greene had lived in Mulberry Grove after the Revolutionary War, but died shortly after. Lazarus, who was given his freedom after the war, chose to return to Mulberry Grove, the only home he ever knew, and was surprised to find that the plantation had been given to Nathaniel Greene by the new government for his contribution in winning the war. The general welcomed Lazarus and employed him as the blacksmith. After the general's sudden death, his widow, Catherine, continued to use Lazarus' services until she sold the plantation in 1800. Lazarus decided to stay on with the new owner. "Git all your work done afore nine tomorrow and we be all set to go, and nobody will miss us if the bales of hay are all in the barn. Git your black ass goin' afor the sun rises," Samuel ordered and added, "I'm goin' to see me this French hero."

Leroy interrupted. "Don't worry your head none about me, I'm gonna be there."

After the boys left, Lazarus continued forging horseshoes, swinging his hammer until the sinews in his muscles bulged from the continuous motion. His thoughts went back to the days he served the Marquis as an aide. He was responsible for the condition of his horse and anything else Lafayette needed. At first Lazarus was reticent to speak to him, but as the days went by he found Lafayette very approachable. He was very appreciative of how Lazarus tended to his horse and kept his sword in excellent shape. Many times he asked Lazarus about himself. Lazarus found himself telling his life story. How his mother was born in Mulberry Grove, Georgia, on a plantation owned by James Bulloch. When he was born, his mother didn't think he would live because he didn't cry right away, and she thought for sure he was dead. When he finally did cry, she exclaimed, "Lordy, Lordy, he came back from the dead." Hence, his given name had to be Lazarus. Early on in his life, his mother made sure that he would have a decent existence. That meant he had to learn to be useful in the white man's world. She would drop him off at the blacksmith's forge on her way to the fields and instruct him to watch and learn. This he did. Before long the blacksmith took notice of him and began teaching him the trade. His owner took notice of this as well and didn't insist on him working in the fields. After Lazarus' teacher died, Lazarus was instructed to choose among the young black men whom he thought were physically fit and intelligent enough to learn the trade as well.

When the Revolutionary War started, Lazarus ran away to join the Continental Army. Because of his skill as a blacksmith, Washington enlisted his services, and when Lafayette joined the Continental Army, he assigned Lazarus to him. Lafayette would talk for hours to Lazarus about liberty for all men including slaves.

"I'm sure when this war ends the new government will attempt to free all the slaves as well." The Frenchman attempted to convince Lazarus of this.

"I shure hopes so. But I has to see it before I can believe it." Lazarus couldn't believe white people would ever mention equality between blacks and whites, not after what he had experienced in his lifetime.

After the war, he was issued his free papers for service in the army and he returned south to Mulberry Grove in Georgia and was employed as a blacksmith in the employ of Nathaniel Greene.

Cornelia Greene, the oldest daughter of the general, would stroll out to the blacksmith's forge when Mr. Whitney finished giving her lessons for the day. Cornelia, at twelve, had developed a school girl crush on the young tutor from Massachusetts. She liked following the young tutor in his walks around the plantation after the day's lesson. Mr. Whitney had told Lazarus he had worked at his own forge in New England as a boy and knew how to handle the anvil. Lazarus was flattered with the attention Mr. Whitney showed him and allowed Whitney to use some of his tools. He had an idea for an engine that would separate cotton from the seed. If Lazarus allowed him to use the forge, he would teach him to read and write. Young Cornelia overheard this discussion and reported it back to her mother. Mrs. Greene chastised Mr. Whitney for this because she evidently wanted this project kept secret from others. She made it perfectly clear to him. Lazarus, like Whitney, was an employee of hers. He had no right to share such information with anyone or to offer his service of tutoring free, especially to a black man. Mr. Whitney was taken back by her reaction. She never complained to him about having Lazarus engrave the letter "C" on the diary he gave young Cornelia for her birthday.

The wagon rumbled over the bumpy dirt road and Lazarus smiled. He had been able to keep the Marquis' sword safe all these years and now he could return it to his beloved friend. Just before he climbed aboard, he carefully wrapped the encased sword and placed it right under the driver's seat. The ride into Savannah was a pleasant one and gave thought to other conversations of long ago.

"Would you be willing to go into the British camp and act as a spy for me?" Lafayette posed the question to Lazarus upon coming out of the tent along with several other officers.

"Me? You is askin' me to help fight them Redcoats?"

"Yes, Lazarus, you. I am going to ask William to go along with you so we can be sure one of you will be able to come back if there is any trouble. I will give a horse to William and to you I will give my treasured sword. This will convince the British you are thieves. In doing this for the cause, you and William will have earned your freedom."

"Ya sa, sir, I is willin' and I know William will too." How long ago was that? He wondered if after all those years he would recognize his hero. *I wonder if he will recognize me. It's been a long time.* The two children in the back of the wagon heard Lazarus talking out loud but the rumble of the wheels on the wagon over the dirt worn road would not allow them to understand all that he was saying.

Chapter 5

Elizabeth paid a visit to city hall and inquired about historical board meetings and when and if she could receive a list of such restorations. "Seems to be a lot of interest in all these homes being restored," the clerk said as she ran off copies. "Only yesterday a gentleman asked the same thing," stacking the papers in a pile. Elizabeth tried to act surprised at the clerk's reply about the coincidence, not wanting to let on about the search that was to ensue. She returned to her apartment after gathering the volumes of information on restoration that had been made since 1994. Her two dogs came running to the front door as soon as they heard the key in the lock.

"Get down, get down, or I'll drop all this stuff right on top of you!" she shouted to them, but they just kept running all around her legs and some of the files fell to the floor. "That's it, get away from me." Her voice rose so they both retreated as she gathered up all the records. "Honestly, one would think I was gone for a week. Oh well, I'm sorry," she lamented. "I guess it is strange for you guys being cooped up here while I'm out. I suppose you miss home."

She reached out to the dogs after placing the papers on a nearby table. "Sorry if I was short with you," she said, petting them gently on their heads. "I have work to do and being here beats being in a kennel up north right? Come on, I'll give you a treat," and she headed for the kitchen.

The dogs settled down and Elizabeth started looking into the reams of data on restoration.

"Let's see, here's one on Price Street. Not much square footage to hide anything there, but you never know." She proceeded to read. About an hour or two perusing the documents, she felt hungry. Instead of making lunch for herself she opted to go out.

The weather was a little chilly A few clouds threatened rain so instead of walking to the Six Pence she decided to take her car. Luckily, there was a parking spot outside the restaurant because it started to rain heavily. Not wanting to open her umbrella for the short run to the restaurant, she made a dash for the door. It wasn't quick enough because she got soaked. She brushed her wet hair back from her face and opened the door. Tom and Art Larson were just about to leave.

"Well, well, hello," Art spoke first. Tom followed close behind. "Elizabeth Adams, as I live and breathe." Art moved to one side. "Look who decided to pay old Savannah a visit, Tom."

"Hello yourself." Elizabeth fielded the sarcastic greeting in its stride, turning her face to Tom. Tom's friendly greeting made up for his father's "hello."

"When did you get into town?"

"A few weeks ago."

"Dad, why don't you go on ahead. Elizabeth, may I join you?"

"Sure." By this time they had reached the back of the restaurant and secured a table. Tom pulled out a chair, allowing Elizabeth to sit. "I'm going to the ladies room to see if I can dry out a bit." In the ladies room she attempted to repair the damage done by the rain. "Of all people to meet, oh well." She blotted her face and applied some makeup.

"You look wonderful. New York certainly has agreed with you," Tom said as he pulled out the chair for her.

"Thanks, you haven't changed much either," she said, although she noticed a slight graying at the temple that only added a more distinguished look.

"What brings you to Savannah?"

"I'm following a lead on this so-called discovery of a Revolutionary artifact.

My boss knows I was raised in the antique business down here, and I suppose he thinks I would know how to go about looking up the lead."

"Hmm, is that so. I haven't heard anything. Have you asked your father if he heard anything?"

"Are you kidding? He still holds a grudge against me for leaving so soon after my mom died."

"Gee, that was twenty years ago. You would think he would have mellowed by now."

"I'm glad you have gotten over the way I left you. You were very upset with me remember?"

"Yeah, I certainly was, but after you left the business picked up and my father and I were kept busy." The waiter appeared and took their order. While Elizabeth looked over the menu, Tom glanced at her face and the old feeling he once felt for her started to well. She is more beautiful now than she was years ago. His thoughts were interrupted.

"Are you having anything?" she asked after giving the waiter her order.

"Just a cup of coffee. I can't get over how wonderful it is to see you again."

During lunch they reminisced about old times and found themselves laughing out loud at things they used to do together. When it came time to leave, Elizabeth gave him her cell phone number. He said he would call. Perhaps they could have dinner. Elizabeth was amazed at the way she felt about seeing him and how quickly the two picked up after so many years.

Chapter 6

Elizabeth went back to her apartment after the reunion lunch with Tom and took her dogs out for a walk. She knew she should have continued on with her research, but the lingering warm feelings that arose during the luncheon compelled her to do otherwise. The rain had stopped and she wanted to think more about those feelings, and walking the dogs through Forsyth Park would enable her to do just that.

A slight wind scattered some of the leaves along the walkways of the park, and the two dogs chased after them, sniffing and relieving themselves. There weren't too many people walking except for a few other dog owners, like her. She took the dogs off their leashes.

"Come here, Lady," a voice shouted from behind the azalea bushes at the south end of the park.

By the time Elizabeth reached the end of the park the owner of Lady appeared. "Sorry about that," the handsome, tall, muscular blond man smiled an apology at her. He reached down to collar Lady, patting the animal on the head. "I wouldn't have let Lady run loose like that had I seen your dogs."

"That's OK. I felt the same way since the park seemed pretty empty. They are cooped up most of the day in the apartment and I guess I feel sorry for them and let them have a run every time I get the chance."

"Do you walk the dogs here often?" he asked. Ordinarily she would have welcomed an inquiry by a good-looking guy at such a friendly meeting, but at that moment her thoughts were strictly on Tom.

"It depends," cutting her remarks, thinking he would just walk away with his dog, but he walked beside her and continued the conversation.

"Do you live here or just visiting?" he persisted.

"I'm here on business from New York."

"Me too, I'm from Atlanta." By now she knew he was tiring because his answers started to match her own. They reached Gaston Street and, annoyed at the interruption, she headed toward home while he crossed over Whittaker with Lady.

"How was the trip out to Mulberry Grove?" Benjamin asked Marion when she came into work the day after her visit to check on Stephen's horse.

"It was pleasant but I didn't stay too long. Stephen was right about the rumors. Mr. Butler told me he had realtors out his way questioning not only him but his neighbors about selling. From what I gather he and the others are staying put."

"I wonder if it has anything to do with what was in the *Savannah Morning News* a while ago."

"What was that?"

"Oh it said something like the Georgia Port Authority was going to set aside some acreage at Mulberry Grove and restore it to the way it was shortly after the Revolutionary War because Nathaniel Greene lived there and Eli Whitney invented the cotton gin there. I suppose it would attract a great deal of tourism and create an enormous amount of employment for people in the surrounding areas."

"Is that right? Hmm, wonder if it has anything to do with the business of an artifact being discovered down here?"

"Never entered my mind, Marion, but you may have something there. Well, I have to start cataloguing these first editions that came in from Tennessee the other day. Some of them are diaries kept by people living back in the early 1800s. Possibly there may be a gold nugget in some of the writings."

"Were you able to get a list of recent restorations in Savannah while I was away?"

"Yes, as a matter of fact I did. Let me get them for you. They're here somewhere in this mess on my desk." He lifted a stack of papers and gave them to Marion. "There were about twenty homes restored in the past ten years. Your work is cut out for you."

"Thanks, I'll just take these and go in the back room and see what I can make of them. Will you be all right cataloguing the books and handling the walk-ins?"

"Sure, go ahead, I'll be fine." Marion disappeared into the back of the shop, juggling the huge pile of information.

Benjamin started to unpack the volumes of books. He handled them very carefully because some of them showed wear and tear. Most of them were diaries kept by settlers who settled in Tennessee in the early 1800s. Normally he didn't peruse them for any great length of time, except one volume caught his eye because it was leather bound with an unusual monogram or logo. It had the letter "C" embossed deeply into the grain almost as though it had been forged into the grain. He opened it to a page and started to read:

Today, I heard Mr. Whitney tell Lazarus he would teach him to read and write in exchange for the use of the forge. They were getting along so well that Mr. Whitney told him to call him by his first name. Imagine that a learned man like Mr. Whitney befriending a ferrier, and a black one at that! I'm going to tell Momma about all I heard. Lazarus bragging about how he served under the Marquis Lafayette. And Mr. Whitney telling him all about the engine he had in mind. How could a black man have any friendship with such a fine gentleman as Daddy's friend? Lafayette visited us when we were in Newport and I never once heard him mention Lazarus' name. I do declare he is a bold face liar. He probably wanted to impress Mr. Whitney.

That was all Benjamin could make out that was legible on the page. He set the book to one side and finished his work on the rest of the books. *Wonder who the author was?* he thought to himself, repeating the passage he had just read in his mind.

Chapter 7

As the wagon approached the city of Savannah, Lazarus noticed people heading toward the riverfront. Most of them were women holding the hands of small children, little boys and girls dressed in blue and white colors significant of the visiting French dignitary. The little girls, many of them not more than three years old, wore colorful sashes and carried baskets of flowers. The little boys wore light blue pantaloons and white vests. The closer the wagon came to the city, the noise and chattering of the multitude caused the two little boys hidden in the wagon to poke their heads out to see.

"Looka all the people. I guess this Lafayette much be as important as Lazarus says he be. We best git out afore he stops somewhere." Leroy stretched his head up and turned to see if this would be a good opportunity to jump from the wagon because all the traffic kept Lazarus busy trying to maneuver the horse away from the crowds. Quickly, the two boys jumped from the wagon, rolled on their sides and stood up, following behind, mingling with the people.

"We has to know where he leaves the wagon so's we can get back home," Leroy said all the while instructing his friend, "You stay close to me so's we don't get lost." Lazarus realized the closer he got to the city the more difficult it would be for him to continue on, so decided to head down Drayton Street to City Market where provisions were made for leaving wagons for farmers. He pulled into an area where several other wagons were and tied his horse to a stanchion. The two boys hid themselves out of Lazarus' view but watched just where the wagon was left. They then scurried away, getting lost in the throng of people.

Lazarus lifted the sword from under the seat and carefully wrapped it in a burlap bag and hoisted it over his shoulder. He followed the crowds over to Bull Street where he saw large numbers of people on their balconies shouting as the parade, now in progress, traveled toward Johnson Square. The little girls who he had seen on the way to the parade now lined the street, spewing the flowers held in their baskets, lining the parade route to where the Marquis would participate in the laying of the cornerstone of Nathaniel Greene. Lazarus was overwhelmed at the public display of affection for his friend, and tears streamed down his face as he proceeded along the parade route. When the entourage that included local dignitaries arrived at Johnson Square, a local official addressed the crowd and welcomed the Marquis. He extolled all of his appreciation for him coming so far to honor his fallen comrade. Lazarus listened and, because he was so far away from the speaker, he couldn't make out all that he said, but he knew from the reaction of the people surrounding him it was very complimentary. Every so often the crowd cheered, *"Viva La Marquis! Viva La Marquis!"* When the Marquis rose to address the crowd, Lazarus stretched his head far above the crowd to get a good look at him. He was balding and gray, as he expected, but the eyes and expression on his face as he spoke hadn't changed over the many years. *How am I going to get to him?* Lazarus started to think. *There are so many people here and it is not likely for a black man to just push his way up to the front.*

Just then a man in the crowd yelled, "Stop that thief, he just stole my poke!" All eyes went in the direction of the voice and a split in the crowd enabled Lazarus to walk toward the podium. Lafayette was distracted by the call from the crowd. As he came closer to where the Marquis stood peering out at the crowd, Lazarus called to his long time friend. The Marquis held his hand over his eyes to focus more on the person who called out to him.

"'Marquis Lafayette, it's me. Remember me, Lazarus?" Some of the men on stage tried to stop Lazarus from approaching further, but the Marquis interfered.

"Lazarus, it's you, you're safe; you made it through. Come here, my friend, come up here, my friend. So many years have passed. How have you been? I'm sure you are a free man. You have served your country well. It must have been difficult getting back from the British. Did the other man make it as well? What was his name?"

"No, sir, William was shot when we was trying to escape, but I was able to git back and I had some papers I stole and gave them to officers in charge. By then they told me you was gone. I gots your sword. I watched when they took it away from me and just where they hid it so when I freed myself I crept back into where they put it and found papers lying on a desk so I took them too."

"What a brave man your are." The Marquis hugged his old comrade and Lazarus felt a great sense of pride in this reunion. "And for your bravery I wish for you to keep my sword as a fond remembrance of me and this occasion. Since the sword was a symbol given to me by your country for my service, it should be only fitting you should be rewarded for yours."

Lazarus couldn't believe his ears. He was to have for his very own this wonderful gift from his friend. The dignitaries on the podium wondered about this scene, but because of the decorum of the Marquis and the behavior of the black man toward him, they knew it was of a personal nature. The words exchanged between the two lost comrades in arms were not in earshot of anyone. The conversation remained secret between the two.

Chapter 8

The somber crowd standing outside the Cathedral of St. John the Baptist watched silently as the funeral procession left the church. Whispers of "Who would ever have thought," and "You never know," could be heard in the large number of mourners. Art Larson had lived in Savannah all of his seventy-five years, and his antique business had been in his family for over a hundred years. He was old money. News of his death flashed on the local news two days before. He had suffered a massive heart attack. Mourners who followed the casket walked quietly to their parked cars on Harris Street. As the funeral cortege slowly pulled away, the trail of cars followed.

   Tom Larson and several relatives stood at the gravesite while the Monsignor read over the deceased. As the coffin was lowered into the grave, Elizabeth, who had been standing in the rear, walked slowly up and stood beside Tom. She reached for his hand and he turned to look at her. Tears welled in her eyes when she saw the sorrowful expression on his face. Neither spoke.

"He seemed fine Friday night at the meeting; in fact, he welcomed me as a new business owner to the community and introduced me to many business owners," said Kathleen Bove, owner of the newly restored Le Provence Bed and Breakfast on Gaston Street. Kathleen was talking to Jane King, the Secretary of the Downtown Neighborhood Association, one of the people she had met at its monthly meeting.

"Yes, it came as a shock to all of us. Art was up for nomination as President for the DNA next year; it's a shame. Excuse me, I want to speak to Tom, Art's son, and offer him my condolences." Kathleen surveyed the mourners gathered in the 1790 restaurant. At the graveside Tom invited all present back to the restaurant for refreshments. She hesitated for a moment but then she thought, *No, he asked everyone, and I did meet him even if it was only once.* Tom stood in a circle surrounded by people, Elizabeth not far from his side.

"It seems we meet too often at such sad occasions," Elizabeth said to Tom as they both walked away from the group. "Was your father complaining about any health problems?"

"No, not really, but he did seem preoccupied about something. I remember one evening when I dropped by to see him after I came back from New York; we had a drink together at the house. He asked me to stay awhile. I declined, but now that I think of it he seemed like he would like to have discussed something with me."

"Do you think it was about the business?"

"I really don't know. I guess I'll never know." He sat down in a nearby chair, looking down at the floor. Elizabeth pulled a chair over beside him and grasped his hand.

"Don't blame yourself. There isn't anything you could have done. I know when my mother died suddenly there was this feeling of guilt. What could I have done differently? It may have seemed callous of me leaving so soon after she died, but both my mother and father knew I was just waiting for an opportunity to get out of Savannah. Your father had a wonderful life in a town that he loved. He had a thriving business and loved having you as his partner. I'm only too glad I am here for you now." Tom looked at Elizabeth and she stroked his face gently.

"I'm sorry to intrude, but someone told me you were Art's son; my name is Kathleen Bove. I met your father last Friday at the DNA meeting. He was so kind. I'm a new business owner in town and he took me under his wing and introduced me to some business owners; my deepest condolences for your loss." Tom rose from the chair.

"Thank you; this is Elizabeth Adams." Elizabeth stood and shook Kathleen's hand. Tom told Kathleen that her father had an antique business in Savannah as well

"Oh, I don't remember the name. Was he at the meeting on Friday?"

"I really can't say. I don't live here anymore. I'm down here on business from New York." Other mourners gathered around Tom. Elizabeth and Kathleen backed away so they could speak to him.

"What kind of business are you in?" Elizabeth asked.

"I just restored a Bed and Breakfast on Gaston Street. My husband and I had an Inn in New Hampshire and after our divorce I decided to strike out on my own but in a warmer climate." *She's quite pretty*, thought Elizabeth, *probably that's why that lecherous old windbag squired her around at the meeting.* Elizabeth may have said all those comforting things to Tom, but she remembered her father had sore dealings with the late Art Larson. She noticed neither her father nor Marion were in the restaurant, although she spotted both of them in the back of the church. Kathleen spoke about how she loved Savannah and hoped the bed and breakfast would be a success.

"Will you excuse me?" Elizabeth broke into the conversation. "I see someone over there I would like to speak to." Kathleen stopped mid sentence and nodded.

Elizabeth wanted to be at Tom's side and skimmed a look over the room to locate him. He had just sat at a table. She walked hurriedly through the mingling throng.

"Have you eaten anything?"

"No, but I'm going to now. How about you? Why don't you sit here and grab something as well."

"Good idea. I am hungry. You stay put. What would you like? They have set up quite a buffet; looks like salads, chicken."

"Anything, whatever you decide." Elizabeth went over to the buffet table and started to fix two plates.

"Hello, Ms. Adams," a voice from behind spoke. She turned around. A look of shock came over her face.

"Charlie Pickett, what are you doing here?" she said angrily.

"Came to offer my condolences, and I might ask the same of you. There was no great love between your family and Art Larson." Elizabeth flung slices of meat on the plate along with some rolls and moved quickly along the table, all the while Charlie Pickett trailed behind. She wanted to get away from him as soon as possible.

"Would you believe who is here, Tom?"

"I really don't know a lot of these people. My father had dealings with many I never met."

"Charlie Pickett, that's who."

"Charlie Pickett, that thief. What in the world is he doing here? My father told me years ago he was finished dealing with him after the forged Jefferson Davis diary. Its providence was questionable, then to make matters worse pawning it off on your father."

"I remember that well; it happened just before my mother died. When he sold it as authentic and the purchaser came back and threatened to sue, it cost my father a great deal of money to settle out of court. Probably that added to the animosity he felt when I left. I can't stand the sight of him. What do you suppose he is up to? I don't think he would mourn his own mother."

Marion and Benjamin returned to the shop after the funeral. Marion didn't want to go but Benjamin said it wouldn't look too good for them, what with being in the same business and all. They decided to attend the funeral mass but leave out the cemetery.

"I'm glad we went. Did you see Elizabeth there? She must have hooked up with Tom since she arrived. She was speckled there among the close relatives. I suppose she'll disappoint Tom again like she did the last time." Benjamin's hostile tone bit the air.

"Who knows, maybe they will get together. He's a nice guy and, like they say, one can't choose your relatives. After that Davis forgery Tom couldn't haven't been nicer, saying he was so sorry about what happened. When he explained they had providence, his father must have held back on some important information. I don't think Tom is anything like his father."

"Maybe not; all I know is it cost me fifteen thousand dollars and hastened Sarah's death. That's something I will always remember."

Chapter 9

Two weeks had passed since Art Larson's funeral. Elizabeth insisted on helping Tom out at the store and also with mailing out acknowledgments to the many mourners who expressed their sympathy. Her work, searching records for the so-called "artifact," she put on the back burner. Tom asked her to move into his father's house so she could have access to the courtyard for the dogs. She declined the offer, knowing the gossip that would ensue. After all, her father lived in Savannah, and she didn't want to cause him any more hurt than she already had.

"That's the last one," Elizabeth said, brushing her hair away from her face. Tom watched her as she lined all the envelopes on the dining room table.

"Thanks, you did a great job."

"*We* did a great job," she quickly replied, and then she glanced over at all the unopened mail at the end of the table. "You had better get to opening all that mail or your lights and water may be turned off."

"This is something I'm going to hate doing. I didn't handle this end of the business. Letter writing is not my strong suit."

"Well, it has to be done. I would offer to help but I really don't know what would be personal so you'll have to just dig in. I have to call my boss and tell him there was an emergency for me so he will understand the delay in reporting. If you would like, I'll come over this evening and cook dinner."

"I'd like that, and thanks for all your help. I should be finished with all this stuff by then. Yes, I'd like that very much."

Elizabeth picked up her coat and pocketbook from a chair and left. Tom grabbed a handful of mail and headed for the kitchen. The usual junk mail was mixed among utility and tax bills. There was one letter with the logo of a detective agency, Fenders and Co Inc., whose name Tom recognized. It was an agency the business used to help establish providence of certain artifacts that had dubious ownership. *Wonder what Dad was trying to find out? I don't remember him telling me about this search and what article it could be. Oh well, stop wondering and open the damn letter.*

Dear Mr. Larson:
Our firm has searched for over two years trying to locate the original ownership of the Revolutionary War artifact you shipped to us. It has been an impossible task. We have met with dead end after dead end. We therefore find it necessary to ship it back to you upon receipt of our services of $2,500.
Yours truly
Jack Fender
Fenders & Co

"I'll be a son of a bitch. Now I know why Charlie Pickett was at his funeral. And after he promised me he wouldn't go near that rotten thief again. What a mess this has made." His anger now replaced the distress he felt up until then. Thoughts of what Elizabeth had said at the restaurant came to mind. *What if she thinks I had something to do with this? Will this send her high tailing back to New York with a story and my chance of ever getting back with her killed? Was that the something he wanted to discuss with me that night I stopped in? Why didn't I stay? Dammit why didn't I stay?*

Charlie Pickett tried to figure out how to approach Tom Larsen. With Art Larsen's death there was no way of finding out how much Tom knew about the sword if anything. Blackmail crossed his mind if Tom pulled the high and mighty like he did with the Davis diary. How would he like his father's name dragged in the mud along with his if Tom didn't pay him a nice hefty figure for the sword? He would wait a week or two until after the funeral and then approach Tom. By then maybe the deal he made with Art would come to light as Tom went through the business records.

"Hello, Tom, this is Charlie Pickett." The sound of the voice on the other end of the phone made Tom start pacing the floor.

"You son of a bitch, what was going on between you and my father? I thought our business was finished a long time ago." Charlie soon realized he had a fight on his hand.

"Your father and I had a business arrangement; no need for name calling. If you'd like, I'll come over and discuss it with you at your convenience."

"You can come over, but I'm sure there will be no business between you and me. I'll be at my father's house around four this afternoon. Be there." He then slammed the phone on the receiver.

Elizabeth had called Marion soon after the funeral and they arranged to have dinner at the Pink House.

"It's a shame about Art Larson's death, it being so sudden and all," Marion said while the waiter poured water in the glasses, asking about cocktails.

"Yes, it's kind of spooky. I mean me being here when it happened. It brought so many memories back about my mother's death."

"All the same, I bet he was glad you were here. You certainly were a comfort to him. Any luck on your research about the artifact? Your dad and I haven't had much and we have been reading about umpteen restorations. Maybe it is a document of some kind, like a diary or a letter written by Washington or Adams? What do you think?"

"Could be. To tell the truth, after his dad died I didn't too much looking. I've been helping him out with his thank you notes and just being there for him."

"I'm sure he appreciates that. Do you think you two will ever get back together? You were pretty tight once and he hasn't married or dated very much. I know he is a stiff competitor at auctions. Just a few weeks ago he tried to outbid me in New York." Marion mustered up a slight grin.

"We do like each other very much, but I don't know how serious it could get. Enough about me, how are Colleen and Stephen doing?" Elizabeth wanted to change the subject. She didn't want Marion to know just how strong her feelings were for Tom. No, not until she was sure he felt the same way. Right now she felt that it was appreciation on his part and she didn't want to get hurt.

"They are both fine. I saw Stephen not too long ago. He is at Georgetown and I stopped on my way to an auction I mentioned to you before. Colleen is at the Sorbonne studying art. I had a postcard from her the other day. She is in seventh heaven."

"I bet I wouldn't recognize them if I saw them. I've been gone such a long time."

"I don't know about that. Colleen looks a lot like you did at twenty. I have a picture of her. You can see for yourself." Marion rifled through her wallet and took out two pictures of the children.

"I'll be, she does look like me." She laughed. "That's not fair; daughters should look like their mothers."

"Hey, we're all family. In a way I'm glad. Your father simply adores her and it's probably because she does look a lot like you."

"I wonder if my father will ever forgive me for the way I left Savannah. It didn't seem that way when I visited him at the store." Elizabeth twirled the stem of her water glass.

The waiter appeared and sat their meal before them. The conversation flowed about old times and both women laughed about the competition that kept them from being good friends.

The next day Marion told Benjamin about the dinner and mentioned how sorry Elizabeth felt about the way she had left Savannah.

Chapter 10

Kathleen wondered how long the guest from Atlanta would stay at the inn. When he arrived, she inquired but he didn't know how long his real estate business with the Georgia Port Authority would take. Besides, she was the only inn keeper that said she would house Lady and that was a plus. Kathleen told him she hadn't had her grand opening yet and some construction work was still underway. If it would be alright with him, the dog could have access to the courtyard and sleep out there at night. Kathleen had a Labrador herself and sometimes she kept him there as well. If it rained, there was a doghouse Lady could stay in. George Bell never thought he would have been able to pull a deal like this off. Kathleen, however, took a great interest in the handsome business man and had other things on her mind.

"How are things coming along with your business trip?" Kathleen asked as she poured his coffee at breakfast.

"Slow. I thought by now the people I am dealing with would have made up their mind about relinquishing some of the property they said they would."

"That's too bad." She shrugged her shoulders and turned away, smiling at the delay. *Good*, she thought to herself, *maybe now I can interest him in something besides real estate.*

He sat there sipping his coffee and reading the *Savannah Morning News*. When he finished, he mentioned that he would take Lady for a walk in Forsyth Park.

"Mind if I join you? Dakota could use some exercise as well."

"Not at all."

The day was blustery and cool. Falling leaves swirled around the park and the two dogs strained on their leashes to chase squirrels scurrying up and down trees. There were some other dog walkers and joggers in the park as well.

"When are you planning your grand opening?"

"My chef thinks Christmas would be an excellent time, I kind of agree. I could have the inn all decorated and there are a number of tourists that visit during the holiday season."

"I hope I'm finished way before that but the Port Wentworth Council is kind of throwing a wrench in my deal."

"How's that?"

"Oh, it has something to do with restoring a plantation out at Mulberry Grove. Seems the city wants some of the land owned by the Port to be set aside for this project, but our deal was made before the council voted on this. I don't know too much about it except my client is upset because they were planning on a strip mall and now the project has come to somewhat of a dead end."

"I know the disappointed you're talking about. When I first came down here and bought the inn, I kept running into more than enough problems. The previous owner failed to mention a few minor details like a sprinkler system, air conditioning problems, antique plumbing. There was a laundry list a mile long. It really had me depressed. But now, thank goodness, I can see a light at the end of the tunnel." By now the two had stopped at a park bench and were sitting down. The dogs, tired of chasing, sat quietly by their owners. "I can't wait for the grand opening and then I know I'll be on my way. I know you want to get back to Atlanta but maybe you would like to come back for the party. I'll reserve a room for you."

He laughed at the invitation then added, "Who knows, at the rate I'm progressing I may still be here." They both laughed and resumed the walk. Just as they headed toward Gaston Street Elizabeth and her two dogs entered the park. Kathleen recognized Elizabeth from the funeral and spoke first.

"Hello, Elizabeth," Kathleen called over the barking of the dogs. George turned to Kathleen.

"I met her here the other day with Lady," he said to Kathleen. "We never exchanged names; she seemed in a hurry. Do you know her well?"

"No, we met briefly at a funeral the other day. She is on business down here from New York. She is a friend of Tom Larson, the son of Art Larson who passed away. He was an antique dealer. It seems her father is also in the antique business and the families have known each other for years."

"Hi, how are you, Kathleen?" Elizabeth pulled her dogs over to the side. Lady and Dakota raced over, sniffing and wagging their tails. "Seems like a dog party."

"Yeah," George said. "Lady remembers your dogs from the other day."

"Yes." Elizabeth tried to untangle her leashes, annoyed by the encounter. George sensed the annoyance and helped her unravel. Her remark about the dog party sounded more like both he and Kathleen were uninvited guests.

"How is Tom holding up?" Kathleen evidently didn't feel the same about the meeting.

"As well as can be expected; he has to see to his father's affairs and I'm sure that will keep him busy and his mind off his loss for the time being."

"How long are you planning to stay in Savannah?" she continued, but by this time George started to walk ahead with Lady.

Her looks don't match her personality, he thought to himself as he walked away. He never heard her reply to Kathleen's question. When Kathleen finally caught up with him, she apologized for not introducing him.

"No problem, I don't think that woman is very sociable." *Good,* thought Kathleen, *less competition for me.*

Chapter 11

Tom Larsen tried to concentrate on sorting out his father's accumulated mail. He couldn't help muttering to himself, all the while ripping open the envelopes addressed to the business "Larsen and Son, Vintage Antique Dealers."

"Vintage. More than vintage, after I find out just what was going on between that bastard Pickett and Dad." *How could he have gone back on his word? Doesn't he know how long it took for people to get over that lousy deal Adams ended up with? And now with Elizabeth back, will she believe I really had nothing to do with it?*

Four o'clock couldn't come fast enough for the distraught Tom Larsen. He managed to discard a great deal of the junk mail and set aside the small pile that needed responses. The business of sorting helped keep him looking up at the clock on the kitchen wall. Four o'clock came and he headed for the living room. He decided to start a fire instead of turning up the thermostat. "It will be hot enough in here without the help of artificial heat when that bastard arrives." He opened the French doors that led to the courtyard to bring in some wood. Charlie Pickett's car pulled in beside his dad's in the carport in back. "Doesn't want to be seen coming in the front I bet." He piled logs in his arms and went into the living room. Charlie stood at the locked carport and waited for Tom to let him come in.

"Getting ready for the cold weather?" Charlie said, trying to set an amicable tone for discussion.

"Let's cut the formalities and get right down to why you are here in the first place. When did you make this business arrangement with my father and what was the artifact involved?" Tom didn't want Charlie to know about the letter from the detective agency.

"Your dad didn't mention our little business deal? It's been well over three years. He gave me a line that ownership was hard to track down and I would have to wait. I think he was trying to fence it and keep me on the hook." Tom's face reddened and he had to hold back the urge to strike Charlie a blow when he talked in that manner about his father.

"What kind of business?" Tom wanted to find out just what he had stolen.

"You really don't know anything about this? It's kind of hard to believe. You being a partner and all." Charlie was no dope. He knew if Art was telling the truth about search for providence, evidence would show up in the form of billing. He purposely waited these two weeks, hoping this news would come to light. "Come on now, you must know something; if your father was on the level there has to be a bill coming from somebody." Tom hated this man. His way of earning a living disgusted him and the fact that his father helped him in robbing antiques added to his anger.

"You think you're pretty smart don't you?" Tom's voice lowered in order for him to think about what next to say. "What if I told you, I just found out partly about what was going on; what makes you think I won't turn this whole matter over to the police?"

"I guess that's the chance I'll have to take, but I'm a gambler and if it has taken this long for ownership to be found, who's to say you can't prove it; after all, it was done once before." At this last remark, Tom took a swing at Charlie who backed away, knocking over an end table and heading for the door. "I guess you're not interested, but just remember what I said about dragging you and your father's name in the mud. Think it over. I'll call you in a few days when you have cooled off." When Tom picked up the end table and looked up, he was gone.

"Hello, anybody home?" Elizabeth entered Art Larson's house carrying several plastic bags filled with groceries. After Charlie Pickett left, Tom went upstairs to take a shower. That whole ordeal had completely wiped him out. He looked for something to put on of his father's. He found a pair of shorts and a sweater. Elizabeth went into the kitchen and started unpacking. "Oh there you are." She looked over the refrigerator door and saw Tom standing in the doorway. "I see you found a change of clothes. I bought some…" Tom interrupted her and asked her to come into the living room; there was something he wanted to tell her, something very important. "Sure, but can't I just start this first…?"

"No, this can't wait, please." Elizabeth, puzzled by the strange request, shut the door of the refrigerator and followed him into the room. Tom started at the beginning with the letter from the detective agency, the phone call from Charlie, and the recent visit that afternoon.

"What are you going to do? This isn't your fault. You didn't know anything about it. No wonder he was at the funeral. The nerve of that guy. Oh my God, I just thought of something! Revolutionary artifact. I wonder…I wonder if that is the rumor that started up in Christie."

"Let me get the letter from the agency. I put it with the pile of mail to be answered. Here it is, it says Revolutionary artifact but not exactly what. But they will ship it back to me when I send them their fee."

"Knowing how crooked that Pickett is I wouldn't put it past him if he was the one who started the rumor some three years ago. Didn't you say he had given it to your father some time ago? I remember when the Davis diary fraud came to light, he had done something similar and that's how buyers at antique auctions thought there was a civil war artifact down here."

"I remember how your dad got stuck with that forgery and my father was to blame for it. I tried to explain to your father I knew nothing about it, but I don't think he believed me."

"Well, I believed you and still do. But what are you going to do about this? How can we find out where he got the item? I don't think he will volunteer that information without seeing money up front. Perhaps when the agency sends it back to you there will be some clue on the item itself."

"I'll get a check out to them right away. I know you will want to report on this, but for now I would appreciate your not saying anything. At least until I know something about the ownership."

"Of course I will; it will make a great story when the truth is all unraveled and hopefully lands Pickett in jail." She got up from the couch, took Tom's hand and said, "But for now I'm going to make us a pasta dish a la New York style," and both headed towards the kitchen.

Chapter 12

"I wish Colleen could be home for Thanksgiving, but I'll guess I'll have to settle for Christmas." Marion and her uncle were sharing lunch together at the store. The search for the mystery artifact had caused lunches to be eaten fast food style. "Nothing new in anything I looked over in the last pile of restorations. Most houses were gutted down to the bare bones and all I came across were zoning permits being issued for plumbing and electricity."

"Perhaps it was just a rumor. You know how stories can take off and take a spin on its own. I wonder if Elizabeth hit on anything worthwhile." Benjamin's mention of his daughter's name gave Marion the chance she had been waiting for. Ever since she and her cousin had lunch, Marion wanted to approach her uncle about the two of them getting together. With the sudden death of Art Larsen, she felt it would be a shame if father and daughter parted again on such ill feelings. Stephen was coming home for the Thanksgiving holiday and this, she thought, would be a good time to mention she was thinking of asking Elizabeth to spend the holiday with them.

"Well we could certainly find that out if we asked her to share the holiday with us. What do you think?"

"It's your house; I suppose you can invite whoever you wish." It wasn't exactly the response she wanted, but at least he didn't say he wouldn't come to dinner if she did.

"Maybe I'll ask Tom too. They seem to be hitting it off. I'm sure he will not want to be alone. What do you say?"

"As I said, it's your house." Her uncle went to the back of the store, carrying the lunch dishes.

Tom had followed Elizabeth's advice and mailed a check for the detective agency's work on the search for providence. He anxiously awaited the arrival of mail deliveries the next few days. Finally UPS delivered the artifact a few days before Thanksgiving. Elizabeth had called him and asked him if he wanted to spend the Thanksgiving holiday with her family. At first he declined saying he felt awkward and upset about his situation with Charlie Pickett but Elizabeth persisted and he agreed to come. When the carton arrived, he carefully took it into his kitchen and laid it on the table. It took a while to tear open the box. He reached down into the mounds of packing stuff and pulled out a long worn leather case. For a moment he forgot how this artifact came to be in his possession and he felt a rush of adrenalin he normally felt when discovering something of historical value he came upon honestly. *This is fantastic*, he whispered to himself, and pulled the sword from the case. Gingerly, his hands pass over the ornamental sword. "The workmanship, the gold handle, the engraved scenes and the lettering, *In Honour of Lafayette*." He found himself talking out loud. "This is magnificent. Where in the world did that thief steal this from? No wonder they had a time trying to find providence." He stood staring at the artifact as it lay on his kitchen table.

George Bell returned from his meeting with the Georgia Port Authority and found Kathleen saying goodbye to one of her guests. Since his arrival there, the two had shared walks in Forsyth Park with their dogs. He found her fun to be with and enjoyed the time they spent together. Kathleen had hoped his business would continue indefinitely. Ever since her divorce she devoted herself to her two boys, getting them set into schools in New Hampshire. After that she headed south and found the inn she had hoped to restore and retire to. George Bell happened and upset her plans. She found him charming, funny and extremely handsome. They found out they had a lot in common during their walks in Forsyth Park. Now that his business was completed with the Georgia Port Authority, he had second thoughts about leaving. Kathleen stood in the doorway waving goodbye. She turned and saw George standing by the reception desk.

"Hi, how are you? I missed you at breakfast had some early errands to run. Is everything OK?"

"Yes, as a matter of fact my dealings are done here and I'm heading back to Atlanta tomorrow. I'd like to thank you for your hospitality, especially about boarding Lady; it was really nice of you."

"I'll be sorry to see you go, but I meant what I said about the grand opening; you're invited, black tie." She laughed, trying to hide the disappointment she felt. "I thought you would be here for Thanksgiving. My two boys are coming down for the holiday and if you have no plans you're welcome to come for dinner." She felt stupid after she blurted out the second invitation on top of the first.

"Thanks." He smiled. *I think she likes me*, he thought to himself. "As of now I haven't heard from my daughter. She usually invites me if her husband isn't traveling. He's in the insurance business and she tags along, especially if its cities she likes to shop in. I'll give you a call when I get back to Atlanta. I think I'll take Lady for a last walk in the park. Want to come?"

"No, I have some guests arriving in about an hour or so and I want to check their rooms to see if everything is in order." Kathleen was glad she had something to do because of the way she extended invitations to him one after another.

Chapter 13

"That's the last bag of groceries," Stephen called to his mother from the open doorway. "If you don't mind, Mom, I'd like to take a ride out to see Beaumont and visit with the Butlers. I'd like to see how Cindy is making out on her riding lessons. Is it OK? Will you be alright?"

"Sure, you go on ahead; it looks like a perfect day for a ride. Thanks for all your help with the groceries. There isn't much you could do for me around here anyway; most of the hard work is over. I'm so glad you're home." Marion hugged him and planted a kiss on his cheek. "Do you have the keys?"

"Yes, OK, I'm out of here."

She closed the door and headed for the kitchen to unpack the bundles. *I'm so glad Elizabeth said she would come for Thanksgiving dinner*, she thought. *Hopefully, Uncle Benjamin and she will reconcile their differences.*

"Now let's see, I hope I didn't forget anything." The unpacking continued as she checked the list she made. "Oh hell, I forgot the gravy master. I'm going to have to make another trip." She finished putting everything away and decided to relax. "I can pick that up tomorrow, or maybe Stephen can run down to Kroger."

Charlie Pickett hadn't heard from Tom and he was getting anxious. *I guess I'm going to have to prod him a little more. I should have pressed his father more and then I wouldn't have to go through all this crap. That bastard was holding out on me.* Charlie Pickett's phone rang and interrupted his train of thought.

"Charlie, this is Tom. I got the sword back. Where in the hell did you steal this from? You know you could go to jail for this. If you think I'm trying to sell this artifact, you're crazy."

"Now you just wait a minute, your father and I had a deal and if you go to the police I'll tell them you were in on it just like your father was. Do you want that?"

"Listen, you lying bastard, what went on between you and my father has nothing to do with me. I'll find out just where this came from and then we'll see who's going to go to jail." He banged the phone down into its receiver. *What in the hell was my father thinking of? Didn't he know I would never let him do this? Oh how I wish I stayed behind that night. I'm going to have to search everywhere to see if he left any papers that would tell me where the bastard stole it from.*

Stephen arrived at the ranch just as the yellow school bus was pulling away from the front of the Butlers. Cindy stood there looking at Stephen's car that had just pulled up.

"Hi, Cindy, how are you and how's the riding lessons coming along?" He came out of the car, stooped over and took her hand.

"Stephen, just you wait and see me. Come on in." She tugged at his hand, pulling him up the driveway. Just then the front door opened and Mrs. Butler appeared. "Momma, Momma, look who came to see us; it's Stephen all the way from college." Stephen remembered the sad parting at the end of the summer when he had to tell her he had to go back to school and wouldn't be able to teach her anymore. She didn't like it very much and it wasn't until her father intervened and said he would continue to help her that she appeared to be less upset.

"Stephen, what a nice surprise. Come in, won't you? I suppose you want to take Beaumont out for a spell."

"Momma, Momma, can I go out with him please, please? I know I can ride alone now. Daddy let me ride by myself the other day and he rode beside me. Please, pretty please?"

"I don't know, honey. Stephen may just want to be alone with Beaumont; it's entirely up to him, dear."

"That will be alright, Mrs. Butler. I'm sure she will be fine." He hadn't planned on this to be an instruction ride, but when he saw the anxiety and desire in Cindy's behavior he had to let her accompany him.

Cindy ran up the stairway, exclaiming in a loud voice, "I'll be right down; I just want to change my clothes."

"This is very nice of you, Stephen, but my husband tells me she is learning very fast, and she did solo the other day, so hopefully it will be a pleasure for both of you." Stephen went to the barn and it wasn't long before Cindy and her mother appeared. He put a saddle on Beaumont while Cindy pulled a tack down from one of the stalls.

"No, no, Cindy." Mrs. Butler reached out to her daughter, struggling to hold the saddle. "Not that one, honey. Your daddy is the only one who uses that saddle." She took the tack from Cindy. "That's one of his prized possessions," she said, turning to Stephen. "He scours antique shows looking for these old saddles."

"Is that so?" Stephen glanced at the tack and noticed the worn saddle had elaborate designs carved in it. "I hope I didn't take the wrong saddle, Mrs. Butler," he said, looking at his saddle for any such marks.

"No, my husband didn't get a chance to put this one away. All the others in the barn are for everyone's use."

She finished adjusting Cindy's saddle and soon the two were out past the pastures and on a trail. Stephen was surprised at how far his pupil had come.

"I'm proud of you, Cindy; you've become quite the horsewoman." Cindy wasn't interested in any small talk. She concentrated solely on mastering her handling of the mount. They rode and at one time Cindy broke into a gallop for a short while just to show off how much she had learned since he left. "Don't do too much of that," he said after he chased her and pulled her reins. "I know you have improved a great deal but it is a good idea just to take your time. Once you have been out a few times, then it will be ok to gallop some."

"Alright, Stephen, I will. I just wanted to show you I'm not afraid anymore."

"Good girl. Well we have been out an hour, we had better go back." They turned their horses around and headed back to the ranch.

When they had settled the horses in their stalls, Cindy insisted he come and visit.

"Why don't you stay for dinner?" Mrs. Butler asked.

"Yes," interrupted Cindy. "Please, pretty please." The child begged and tugged at his jacket. Mr. Butler came down the stairway just in time to see the scene.

"Stephen, why don't you stay; we would like to hear about what's new in Washington these days, and we have had some excitement around here. I suppose your mother told you all about the realtors being out this way."

"Yes, I was glad to hear the owners weren't interested in selling off their properties."

"That's not entirely true, but why don't you stay for dinner and I'll fill you in on all the details."

Stephen agreed but said he would like to call his mother and tell her. Mr. Butler, Stephen and Cindy went into the living room while Mrs. Butler headed for the kitchen.

Chapter 14

"That was delicious, Mrs. Butler; it's nice to have home-cooked meals again."

"Thank you, Stephen; how about some dessert…I have pie a la mode, jello?"

"No thank you. I couldn't eat another thing. That roast beef did the trick for me; I'm not able to manage another bite. So there was a lot of other information surrounding the Georgia Port Authority's decision on the land sale out at Mulberry Grove." Stephen addressed his last remark to Mr. Butler.

"I found out about that when I had lunch with a neighbor of mine last week. It seems his son is a security guard who works for the Georgia Port Authority. About three years ago his son discovered a break-in out at the area surrounding the old Nathaniel Greene site. The plantation isn't there anymore. It was burned down during the Civil War but a blacksmith's forge is still there. That particular area is protected by the Mulberry Grove Foundation as a historic site. Hopefully, the Foundation can restore the original plantation since there is quiet a bit of history there. Washington visited Nathaniel Green's widow and Eli Whitney invented the cotton gin there."

"Is that a fact? I didn't know that. What happened to the rumor then?"

"The son said that some thieves were periodically sneaking in and digging around the forge foundation. The Georgia Port Authority fenced the property in to prevent any more thieves from getting in, but they never found out if anything was taken."

"How about that?" Stephen said, rising from his chair. "I must be getting on home." He looked at his watch. "My mother is having company for Thanksgiving. My Aunt is down from New York. I suppose my mother will need some help for the day. Thanks again."

Cindy ran over to him and gave him a hug. Mrs. Butler wished him a wonderful holiday. Mr. Butler walked him to the front door.

"Don't worry about Beaumont, we'll take good care of him," called Mrs. Butler from the dining room.

"Thanks again," he said and left.

Tom called Elizabeth after he had called Charlie Pickett. He was very upset and asked her to come over. "A sword that belonged to Lafayette, how in the world did that ever land in Savannah?"

"I don't know; all I know is this is some mess my father left for me to clean up. Can you come over? It's a beautiful piece but I haven't got a clue where it came from. And I'm sure Charlie Pickett isn't about to tell me either. It's a long story, can you come over?" Elizabeth sensed the anger in Tom's voice over the phone.

"Sure, would it be alright to bring the dogs? I have to walk them."

"Of course, you can put them in the courtyard. I hate to bother you with all of this but maybe you and I can sort this thing out." Elizabeth felt sorry for Tom but was glad he asked for help.

"I'll see you in an hour or so. Meanwhile start looking through business correspondence and the like. Something might turn up to give us some kind of clue as to where it came from."

"Ok, I'll get on it right away." He placed the phone on the receiver and went into his father's den where he kept all his papers, and started sorting out things.

Elizabeth collared her two dogs and headed out to Forsyth Park. "This is going to be a very short walk," she said to the dogs as she walked down Jones

Street. "My Tom needs me." She smiled to herself. "I like the way that sounds; my Tom."

Stephen hugged his mother from behind as she stood at her kitchen sink peeling potatoes. The counter top was lined with vegetables, pots, and serving dishes. "Stop that," she said as he reached for some celery sticks she'd arranged in a relish dish. "That's for tomorrow." Stephen stepped back quickly but didn't relinquish the sticks in his hand.

"I thought I couldn't eat any more after that roast beef dinner Mrs. Butler put out. It was awesome but I just couldn't resist."

"Don't sample anything else then; just take those. Besides the great dinner out there, how are Beaumont and Cindy?"

"Cindy is doing great. In fact, she rode out with me and spooked me when she took off in a gallop. Her father has really worked with her. We had a great time."

"Any more talk of condominiums being built out there?"

"No, as a matter of fact Mr. Butler told me a story about some thieves stealing artifacts out of property owned by the Georgia Port Authority." Stephen went on and gave his mother all the details Mr. Butler had related to him.

"Hmm, wonder if those thefts have anything to do with the rumor about the Revolutionary artifact."

"What rumor?" Stephen asked. Marion didn't want to discuss the reason why his aunt was in Savannah. The thought did cross her mind that Stephen's story may have something to do with it, and she didn't want it to become fodder for the Thanksgiving Day holiday dinner.

Chapter 15

When Elizabeth arrived at the Larson house, Tom was in his father's den opening the desk drawers. Papers were strewn about on the top of the desk and file cabinet doors were opened.

"What a mess. I haven't found anything that would tie into the sword."

"There has to be some evidence of the transaction. I think your father would have kept something. Let's go through all of this slowly."

The two of them rummaged through old bills, receipts and newspaper clippings for several hours.

"This is hopeless. I guess he knew if I found out about his deal with Pickett I'd blow my stack. That's why there isn't anything."

"Hold on, let's look at some of these old newspaper clippings."

"I don't think they would tell us anything. He used to cut out our paid ads. Kind of stupid I think. But he said he wanted to be sure the paper spelled our name right."

"You never know. Wait a minute, this isn't an ad about the store. Look at this, Tom. It's a clipping about the Port Authority and how they plan to restore the old Nathaniel Greene plantation out at Mulberry. And here is another one all about thieves stealing artifacts and the Port Authority is going to put a fence around it. That's it. Pickett must have stolen it from the site and your father couldn't resist the temptation to cash in on it."

"I'll be a son of a bitch. I bet you're right. That's why the agency couldn't trace providence on it. The engraving on the sword threw them off. I suppose when they ran into dead ends in this country it would have cost more than my father would have paid for them to continue a search out of the country. That's why they asked to be paid up front for the work already done. If my father wanted to continue on, he would have had to pay for the work they had done up to now."

"Well at least we know where it might have come from. You will have to let Pickett know where it was stolen from. What do you intend to do about it?"

"Give it back to the Georgia Port Authority. I don't want anything to do with it. Hopefully they won't do anything to me. Knowing Charlie Pickett, I don't think he will want to go to jail. If he threatens to tell the police about the deal he made with my father, I'm going to tell the Georgia Authority who stole it."

"Good. Now that that's done, can I have a peek at the treasure? After all, that's why I came down here."

"It's inside on the dining room table. I'm curious myself, how in the hell did it land in Savannah?"

"Well, Lafayette did help us during the Revolutionary War. I remember that because of an essay I wrote way back when. Never forgot it. My cousin Marion placed first in a competition the *Savannah Morning News* ran."

"I remember how competitive you both were back in those days." Tom managed a wry smile. Elizabeth was glad she could take his mind off his ordeal for a while. They both went into the dining room and Tom took the sword out of the leather case.

"Oh my, it's beautiful," exclaimed Elizabeth. "No wonder your father gave into temptation. What an exquisite piece of workmanship. Look at the intricate carvings and the detail work on the handle. I bet that would go for an easy million dollars."

"I'm sure you're right in that respect. Too bad my dad didn't come by it honestly." Tom replaced the artifact back into its case and sat down on one of the dining room chairs. Elizabeth could see the disappointment in his face. He dropped his head and cupped his face in his two hands.

"It's not your fault, Tom. Please, please try and remember that."

Elizabeth knelt down to his knees and touched the top of his head. He slowly removed his hands and stood reaching out to her. When they both stood facing each other, he aggressively kissed her. She, in return, hungrily returned the passionate embrace and they clung to each other for a long while.

"Elizabeth is this really happening? Are we back on the same page as we were twenty years ago? I'm so glad you're back, well not really back. I think you have an idea what I mean. Ever since the day I saw you in the restaurant I was hoping something like this would happen. Do you have that same kind of feeling?" Elizabeth pulled back and tried to gain some composure after the surprise embrace.

"Yes, me too; after seeing you I went back to my apartment. I was so confused I took the dogs out for a walk to think. I couldn't even work at the project I was sent here to do. You appeared to be the same, well maybe with the exception of a few distinguished gray hairs." She smiled. "The clock seemed to have stopped while we were talking that afternoon, and I felt as if it was just like us having dinner at the Six Pence so many years ago. It must be something about Savannah remaining caught in a time warp, what with all the history that surrounds it."

"Well, for whatever reason that drew you to Savannah, I'm glad. Where do we go from here?"

"Right now let's figure out a way for you to get out of this mess." "You're right." By this time his demeanor had lightened up and Elizabeth went on to mention
that it would be good getting out for Thanksgiving dinner at her cousin Marion's.

"You may think it's childish on my part, but knowing what I know about the sword gives me an edge on discovery. This gives me a certain edge on Marion. She told me they hadn't found anything in their search for the 'so-called artifact rumor.' When we had lunch the other day we kidded each other about the competition between us as kids. I'm glad we are able to do that now. If only my father could find it in his heart to forgive me, this would be more than what I had hoped for in my return."

"Maybe seeing you in a social situation among family, it just may happen. We'll see on Thursday. I wish I could tell him about this mess I'm in and tell him my intentions of returning it to the rightful owners. Who knows, he may then find it in his heart to forgive my entire family."

Elizabeth agreed and the two of them decided to make plans for dinner and discuss a course of action that would lead to the return of the sword.

Chapter 16

The crowd had reassembled back in front of the podium after a policeman took pursuit after the accused thief in the crowd. By this time the conversation between Lafayette and Lazarus had ended. Lazarus stepped down from the podium and he soon melted into the sea of people. Not only the dignitaries on stage noticed this poignant meeting.

"Do you see what I see?" Leroy, wide eyed, stared at his friend, Samuel.

"I sure do. What in the world is Lazarus doing up there with that there man? He best get down from there. Looka. Those other men is goin to grab him."

"No, wait a minute, they is stoppin' from goin' over to where he be."

"That there Marquis is huggin' and kissin,' what in the world. It must be true what Lazarus has been tellin' us about him being a friend of his. I'll be."

"Look, Lazarus is taking somethin' out of that sack he done be carrying. I can't see too good." Just then the crowd started to push their way up front to better see the hero after the commotion caused in the crowd.

"C'mon, let's be goin' afore Lazarus sees us and we git a wallopin.' I wonder what it be that was in that sack." The two boys wove their way through the throng of people and headed back to where the wagon was. "Good, he not be back yet, there is the wagon."

They made a dash for it and quickly jumped in under the cover in back. It wasn't too long after it they heard Lazarus boarding the step that led to the driver's seat. The two boys were very silent, still in shock about the scene they had witnessed at the ceremony.

"C'mon, ole Bessie, we best be getting home. This has been the happiest day of my life. My hero done give me the treasured sword of his, I'll be." He laughed out loud, raised the reins and slapped the horse to a start. The two boys heard what Lazarus said, and because they didn't want to get caught just stared at each other with mouths and eyes wide open.

Upon arrival back at Mulberry Grove, Lazarus drove the wagon to the back of the forge. He stepped down and removed the sack containing the sword. There wasn't anyone around and he knew this treasure had to be hidden. His story would hardly be believed by the white folks. After all, he knew what happened when Mr. Whitney taught him to read and write. *That Mrs. Greene sure wasn't too happy. And after me doing that decoration for her daughter, Cornelia's, book. No, them white folk would sure take this away from me. I has to find a hiding place.* The two boys waited until Lazarus was inside the forge to alight from the wagon.

"How's about that?" Samuel said to Leroy as he helped him down quietly from the wagon. "He has himself a sword that belong to a hero." The two boys didn't notice Lazarus coming up behind them.

"What you boys doin' in my wagon?" Startled, the boys wheeled around to face a very angry Lazarus. Samuel, the older boy, jumped in front of his younger friend, trying to protect him from the swing of Lazarus' arm. Samuel ducked just in time, but in doing so Leroy fell to the ground. "I askin' you what you all doing in my wagon?"

Both boys cowered at the wrath spewed forth and stuttered over how they hid in the wagon because they wanted to see his hero. Samuel somehow mustered up enough courage to challenge the older man by saying he saw and heard what went on between him and Lafayette. When Lazarus heard this, his voice toned down. "You saw the Marquis and heard what he said?"

"No," a shaken Samuel said. "We saw you gettin' up on that stage. We thought for sure you was a goin' go to jail, but then the fussin' in the crowd was not on account of what you did but some stealin' goin' on. We couldn't hear but we saw, and then when you was a climbin' and getting in the wagon you talking all about the sword. It all be true what you be tellin' us, you sure is a hero to us too." Lazarus gained composure after the boy explained and told them both that they had to promise to keep it between the two of them, and in return he would teach them both to be blacksmiths. In time he said he would also teach them to read and write as well. Both boys were delighted with this agreement and promised they would never ever tell a living soul.

As years went by both Samuel and Leroy learned to be blacksmiths and Lazarus secretly taught them both how to read and write. One thing he never revealed was just where he had hidden the precious gift.

Chapter 17

Marion had asked Stephen to go to Kroger and pick up the gravy master she had forgotten. She intended to do it earlier but had gotten involved in house cleaning and didn't want to shower and change.

"Not a problem, Mom," Stephen shouted over the noise of the vacuum cleaner. "Is there anything else needed for the big day?"

"No, I don't think so. If you see anything else you may want just pick it up."

"OK." Stephen left and headed down to Kroger. The day was warm but not humid as it had been all that summer. The temperature hovered around seventy-five degrees. People were walking dogs in nearby squares as usual. *I love this town*, thought Stephen. *Too bad Mom doesn't have a dog. It would be company for her while Colleen and I are away at school, but then with her traveling as much as she does on buying trips. I suppose she feels it wouldn't be fair to the animal. I hope Aunt Elizabeth brings her two dogs tomorrow. Aunt Elizabeth, heard a lot about her from Uncle Benjamin. Mom never comments though when he gets on her case. Wonder what she looks like? I have always wondered why she never came to visit; maybe tomorrow it will be all cleared up.* By this time he had reached Kroger. He headed toward the customer service desk. *I don't want to be wandering around all day up and down the aisles.*

"Excuse me. Could you please tell me where I would find gravy master?"

The woman at the desk glanced over at a cork board with a file attached to it. She flipped through several pages and then said, "Aisle seven."

"Thank you." Stephen turned and felt a hand on his arm. He turned back again and Brother William, an old teacher of his from the Benedictine Military in Savannah, smiled at him.

"Stephen, I see you're home for the Thanksgiving holiday. It's great seeing you. How is everything going at school?"

"Just wonderful, Brother William, couldn't be better. I lucked out and got morning classes so I can make the best of studying during the afternoon. That's why it's great being a senior."

"Glad to hear. Oh, by the way, if you could help me out tomorrow, one of my students had an unfortunate accident at a football game and he won't be able to assist at the annual Thanksgiving Mass at the Cathedral. Do you think you could help us out? We're short."

"I think so; my mother must still have my uniform. I'll let you know. Hope it still fits me. I'll give you a call when I get home." *Nice guy*, Stephen thought as he stood at the check-out line, *but that puts the cabash on my first football game viewing of the day.*

"I think it will fit. I put it in the back of your closet. Take it out and try it on. It will have to be aired out. It's been in that plastic wrap since you went away to Georgetown." Stephen's mother was delighted at the chance meeting with Brother William. She had been thinking of asking Elizabeth and Tom to join them at the ten o'clock mass on Thanksgiving Day, and this would be perfect, she thought. The uniform fit accepts for the length. Marion said it wouldn't be a problem because there was a hem she could let down and press.

"I'll give Brother William a call. I suppose the number hasn't changed. Is it in your phone book?"

"Let me see. It should be here. Yes, here it is." Stephen called and was glad he could accommodate his old high school teacher. Marion spent most of the rest of the day washing the shirt and letting down the hem. When she finished and admired her handy work, she sat down and dialed Elizabeth's number.

"Hello, Elizabeth, it's Marion. I was wondering if you would join us at the ten o'clock mass in the Cathedral tomorrow. We usually attend and this year is kind of special. Stephen was asked by an old high school teacher of his from the Benedictine Military Academy if he would serve. I don't know whether or not you would like to but I thought I would ask anyway. You could ask Tom to join us as well."

"I would like that very much. I don't know about Tom but I certainly will come. He has been very busy straightening out his father's affairs. There is one mess in particular. I hope it all works out well for him. This would be good for him, take his mind off of business for one day at least. Sure, I'll ask him, but in the event he declines, I'd love to go. I'm looking forward to seeing Stephen."

"We'll pick you up at nine thirty. What's your address?"

"No need. I'll walk over and wait for you in front of the church. See you tomorrow."

Chapter 18

Tom accepted the invitation to go to mass on Thanksgiving from Elizabeth. He thought it would be a peaceful way to start the holiday and possibly ask for divine intervention for the predicament his father left him. Thanksgiving Day arrived slightly overcast. Temperatures had fallen to the low seventies. It felt good after all the intense heat of the last three months. The smell of fall was in the air. Elizabeth said everyone was meeting in front of church about nine thirty. Benjamin had arrived first at the church and was pacing up and down when Marion and Stephen arrived.

"Elizabeth hasn't gotten here yet," Marion said, glancing toward Jones Street. "I wonder if Tom is coming. I thought it would be nice asking him to join us since he's coming to dinner."

"I'd like to stay and say hello to Aunt Elizabeth, but I had better get inside."

"You go on ahead; we'll see you later," said his mother. Stephen dashed around the corner to the chapel entrance on Harris Street. Elizabeth and Tom came strolling down Lafayette Square, chatting and smiling at each other.

"Looks like they have picked up where they left off," Benjamin said, climbing the church steps, not waiting to greet them.

Marion waited and waved, acknowledging their arrival. *Hope the rest of the day goes better than this,* she thought to herself.

"What a wonderful day weather-wise; you can smell fall in the air can't you?" Elizabeth shouted as she crossed over Harris Street.

"It sure feels that way," responded Marion. "Tom, I'm so glad you came. I suppose Elizabeth told you Stephen was asked to volunteer to assist at mass."

"Yes she did; brings back a lot of old memories about the BMT for me. We all had a turn as altar servers. It's a nice tradition that has passed down from generation to generation, isn't it?"

"I think so, but personally I think Stephen wanted to go to his old high school football game. Maybe in time he will appreciate the tradition." Marion laughed. "Ever since 9/11 attendance at this particular service has increased. I suppose our country realizes we are not all that safe from those who hate our ideals."

Tom felt uneasy when Marion mentioned the word "ideals." Thoughts about the theft of the sword surfaced and made him uncomfortable. He glanced up to where Benjamin stood and noticed Benjamin's icy stare at the group. Benjamin waited at the entrance of the church. Marion walked past Benjamin, then Tom shook Benjamin's hand and Elizabeth smiled a greeting to her dad. The group then entered the church and walked down the center aisle and luckily was able to find an empty pew that would accommodate them. All during the mass Tom felt uneasy and prayed. As he saw Stephen walking down the aisle, he recalled his high school days. In those days he and Elizabeth were inseparable. He never thought she would leave Savannah, but now with her by his side he tried to concentrate on solving his father's mistake. Elizabeth drifted back to those days as well. She glanced at her father every so often and wished she could have left on better terms. *Maybe Tom is right. Dad is still bitter about Mom's sudden death and how the Davis diary seemed to have hastened it. Now with this horrible Charlie Pickett thing...* Just then the priest intoned:

"And now let us turn to each other and offer a sign of peace." Benjamin felt it was time to forgive his daughter. The sermon the priest gave that day touched Benjamin. He felt that church was the only right place to say "I'm sorry" to her. Years of animosity disappeared as he turned to Elizabeth and said, "Please forgive me." Those unexpected words spoken by her father caught her unaware. Tears welled in her eyes as she hugged and kissed her father. Tom, moved by the poignant scene, turned to Elizabeth and gently kissed her on the cheek. Marion couldn't have been more pleased and smiled.

Chapter 19

Stephen stood at the bottom of the Cathedral steps waiting for his mother. Benjamin stopped to speak to the Monsignor and introduced Elizabeth to him. The Monsignor was surprised. Benjamin had never mentioned a daughter living in New York. The Monsignor thought that Marion and her two children completed his family. Benjamin's resentment toward Elizabeth kept him from ever speaking her name to anyone. All the animosity he felt toward her disappeared at mass that morning.

"Have a wonderful holiday with your family," the Monsignor said. "Don't be a stranger to Savannah. I'm sure your father looks forward to your visits." Elizabeth beamed.

Tom joined in. "I do too," and reached for her hand. She squeezed his hand and the happy group descended the church steps.

"Hi, Aunt Elizabeth." Stephen approached her and gave her a kiss on the cheek. "It's great to finally get to meet the New York branch of the family. For a minute there I thought I was looking at my sister Colleen. The resemblance is awesome. But I guess your father must have told you that."

"No, but your mother called it to my attention at lunch the other day. I told her it wasn't fair. All daughters should look like their mothers. When I look at you though, it makes up for it. You have your mother's eyes and smile. I suppose you're endowed with all her smarts as well." She laughed.

"I don't know about that. I think Coleen is the brains in the family."

Marion just listened to all the banter going on with everyone smiling and laughing. *This is going to be the best Thanksgiving ever. If only Coleen were here, it would be perfect,* she thought.

Elizabeth and Tom said they were going to have breakfast at Clary's. Stephen said he was going to try and catch the end of the football game at the school and hopefully see some old friends. Marion and Benjamin declined the invitation to Clary's. Marion wanted to get home and see about dinner and Benjamin wanted to stop at the store to check on something. Marion told everyone dinner would be about four o'clock.

When Tom and Elizabeth reached Clary's, they had to wait for a table. Tom could see the happiness on Elizabeth's face. "I couldn't believe my ears in church when my father spoke to me. I can't tell you how happy he has made me."

"I'm so glad for you; perhaps now you will be down here more often…not just to see your dad but for us too."

"Right now I'm on cloud nine. I don't even feel like going back to New York…all those years we hadn't talked to each other…what a waste…oh but now I'm so glad that's all behind us. And how I feel about Marion has changed too. Maybe that old adage about time healing all wounds has a ring of truth in it. That feeling of having one up on Marion when I saw the sword Pickett stole from the Georgia Port seems so foolishly competitive given the circumstances of how it was found. In church this morning when I looked at my dad and wished things were different between us, I realized how my father blamed the Davis incident for some cause in my mother's death. How could I have felt this great satisfaction knowing it was caused by something a thief did?"

"Well, at the time you hadn't been reconciled with your father…that possibly could be why. And speaking about the sword, I'm wondering now that there seems to be reconciliation between you two, I'd like to keep it that way. What if at dinner we tell your dad about it? Maybe in this way he will realize all Larsons are not of the same ilk. I don't want any monkey wrenches thrown in about us getting back together. What do you think?"

"It's a great idea, but don't you think you should definitely be sure it came out of the Port Authority first?"

"Those clippings make me almost positive it came from there. When I confront Pickett again, I'll tell him I've told your dad about it, so it may make him back off about blabbing and ruining my name." The waitress placed the check on the table. Most of the patrons had left and they realized the restaurant was closing. "Looks like they just opened for breakfast. I suppose the help wants to get home for the holiday as well. Let's take a walk to Forsyth." By the time the two left the restaurant the sun came out and it was a perfect fall day.

Chapter 20

"Hmm, that smells soo good," Stephen said, taking off his jacket and throwing it on a chair. "I'm starving!" he hollered into the kitchen as he passed the festive dining room table all set with china and a lovely Thanksgiving Day floral centerpiece. "Nobody here yet. I hope everyone comes soon."

"What time is it?" Marion turned around to see Stephen sniffing the turkey on the kitchen counter. "The turkey has been out for twenty minutes. It will be easier to carve if it is a little on the cool side." Stephen glanced at his watch.

"It's a quarter to four. Mom, that smells so good. Can't wait to dig in."

"I'm sure they will be on time; meanwhile, do me a favor. See if there are some empty hangers in the hall closet. If not, would you bring some from upstairs?"

"Will do." He remembered throwing his jacket on the chair in the living room and picked it up before he checked on the hangers. *I guess that's a subtle hint to me to hang up my jacket. Sometimes I think she has eyes in the back of her head,* he thought to himself.

SAVANNAH JOY

The doorbell rang. "I'll get it. Elizabeth and Tom are here. And there's Uncle Benjamin parking his car." Stephen swung the door open to allow them to enter, and stepped outside, waiting for his uncle. "Hi, Uncle Benjamin, glad you were able to park right in front of the house. I know how parking can be one swift pain in the butt." His uncle agreed and they too entered the house.

Elizabeth offered to help but Marion said thanks but everything was done. Marion suggested that Tom play bartender since he brought some assorted beverages. Stephen said he would assist so Elizabeth, Marion and Benjamin sat in the living room. Elizabeth remarked how Stephen looked so much like Marion and how she must be so proud of him. "He certainly has grown up to be a handsome fellow. Can't understand the tricks our genes play on us, but as you said, Marion, we're all family." Benjamin sat quietly observing the two women chatter and then after a while he spoke.

"I'm so glad that you're here, Elizabeth. How can you ever forgive me for being so bullheaded for so long? What a waste of precious time. I was thinking when I went back to the store this morning how your mother would have handled this so differently had the circumstances been reversed. She never would have held such a terrible grudge against anyone for such a great length of time, let alone her own daughter. I took out an old album of pictures of the family when you were growing up here in Savannah. When you stop by at the store I'll show it to you. I spent hours this afternoon just reminiscing about those wonderful days. But enough about what's past." He held his wine glass up and proposed a toast for better days. By then Tom and Stephen came out of the kitchen just in time to hear Benjamin propose the toast. Stephen knew whatever had transpired in the past was now forgotten, and he had no intention of inquiring about what it was.

"I thought you would have brought your dogs today," Stephen said to his aunt. "Bulldogs are my favorite. I suppose it goes with being a Georgian. Speaking of which, there is a game on at six o'clock, Georgia Tech and Notre Dame. I don't know if the ladies are interested, but I know Uncle Benjamin is. How about you, Tom?"

"Count me in, Stephen."

"Let's get through dinner first," interrupted Marion.

"That goes without saying, Mom. Are you kidding?" Marion then left the group and Elizabeth followed her into kitchen.

"Are you sure there's nothing I can do," Elizabeth said.

"I'm going to ask your dad to carve the turkey. Ok, you can help dish out the vegetables into these serving dishes. I'll finish making the gravy." It wasn't long before the sumptuous meal was presented and Marion asked her uncle to say grace.

"Thank you, Lord, for all your bountiful gifts and for giving me back my daughter." It ended with an "amen" by everyone present.

Chapter 21

Marion, Elizabeth and Tom kidded each other about the things they did growing up together in Savannah. Benjamin enjoyed the camaraderie among the three of them. Stephen listened for the greater part and couldn't help interject. "You guys were some wild bunch way back then."

"Midnight in the Garden of Good and Evil hadn't put Savannah in the limelight way back then," chimed in Benjamin. "The town has grown and changed so much in twenty years. I suppose it is for the greater good, but I can't help but feel that people were more neighborly."

"I know what you mean," added Tom, hoping to look for an opening in the conversation to enlist Benjamin's help and support in returning the sword to its rightful owners. "As wild as you think we were, Stephen, the pranks we pulled never caused any harmful damage to any of our neighbors. People were on a first name basis and we knew if we got caught there would be a price to pay. You're right about the change." Tom looked and nodded at Benjamin.

Stephen rose from the table and asked to be excused; he wanted to call the Butlers to see if he had left his cell phone there.

"You must have had it there because you called me from there," said Marion.

"I remember going into the hallway when I called and I thought I put it in my jacket before I took it off and went into dinner. It may have fallen out of my pocket. I never realized I didn't have it until this morning."

"Do you ride out there?" asked Tom. "They're a great couple, the Butlers; I board my horse there."

"You'll be glad to hear then they are not thinking of selling the ranch to realtors. Before I left for school there was a rumor going around that they were."

"Is that so? Funny, I never got wind of that, but glad to hear that news."

"Me too. I would have had to take my horse Beaumont somewhere else, but Mr. Butler told me a neighbor of his filled him in why there was so much interest in the property out at Mulberry." Stephen then related the story about stolen artifacts out at the Georgia Port Authority. Elizabeth stared at Tom and kicked him under the table. Stephen then went to call the Butlers.

Tom looked at Marion and Benjamin at that point and couldn't help but to unfold the terrible dilemma his father had left him. Benjamin cleared his throat and picked up a glass of water. Marion looked over at Benjamin as he rose from the table. He held the glass to his lips and slowly sipped the water. As he placed the glass on the table, he wiped his mouth with his napkin and started to speak.

"Today was one of the happiest days of my life, that is up until this moment." Elizabeth interrupted quickly because she was only too familiar with the look that came upon his face. A look of long ago, when he felt abandoned.

"You have to realize, Dad, Tom didn't know anything about this. He…"

Her father glared at her and said angrily, "How long have you known about this?" He didn't give her any time to respond to his question because he headed for the front door. Marion went after him and brushed against Stephen as he entered the dining room.

"Where's Uncle Benjamin going? What's going on? Why is he leaving?" He called to his uncle but the front door had shut and he was gone. Marion came back into the room and, still in a state of shock on hearing about Tom's situation, sat down and started to ask Tom when did all this start.

"As I told your uncle, this all came to light after my dad's death. Charlie

Pickett filled me in on how this had been going on for three years. When Stephen mentioned the break-in at the Georgia Port, it only confirmed the suspicions Elizabeth and I had. We had found old newspaper clippings my father had kept in his desk drawer."

"I'm in the dark about all this," Stephen said to the entire group. Marion then told him why his aunt was in Savannah and how she was sent down to investigate the rumor in New York about a Revolutionary artifact being discovered in Savannah.

"But why is Uncle Benjamin all bent out of shape?"

"I suppose it brings back some bad memories about a deal my father had with your uncle many years ago." Tom went into detail about the Davis diary. Elizabeth, visibly upset because of her father's action toward Tom on hearing the news, left the table. Marion followed her into the kitchen.

"Oh, Marion, this was such a happy day. If only he'd stayed and listened, he'd realize Tom had nothing to do with it. He doesn't want the damn thing. He intends to give it back. Why couldn't he have listened?"

"I suppose the hurt of long ago resurfaced and he just couldn't face it. Don't worry. I'll speak to him. It will be alright. You'll see." Stephen and Tom came into the kitchen. Elizabeth, still crying, looked at Tom.

"I should have kept it to myself. I'm so sorry, Elizabeth. I shouldn't have involved you and your family in all my trouble."

"It's not your fault. My father will understand once he finds out your intentions. You didn't do anything to be sorry for. It's that…that damn Charlie Pickett who keeps interfering in my life. He's the one I'm really mad at." Marion chimed in, adding she would straighten it out with Benjamin. By this time Stephen disappeared into the living room and left the group in the kitchen.

"What a mess. I hope Uncle Benjamin listens to Mom," he whispered to himself as he tuned in the ball game.

Chapter 22

After Benjamin left, Elizabeth helped Marion with the cleanup. Tom joined Stephen watching the game, but after a short while he decided to head home. He felt embarrassed at the situation he had created and felt guilty about the holiday being upset by blurting out his troubles. Marion understood. He thanked her for the invitation and apologized about ruining her Thanksgiving. Elizabeth walked him to the front door and tried to comfort him as best she could, but he just wanted to leave. He said he would call her in a day or two.

After he left, Marion quizzed Elizabeth about the sword. Elizabeth described it in full detail.

"It's one of the finest artifacts I've seen in a long, long time. The ornamental hand carving indicating battles where he fought are engraved in the handle itself. The workmanship is superb and even the leather casing is so well preserved. I wonder just where it was hidden to have been preserved so well."

"Do you think Tom will let me see it or do you think that would be asking too much?"

"I don't think so. He left because he is embarrassed about all that happened. He thought my father would have been glad to nail Charlie Pickett. After all, he has caused our family a great deal of pain." Stephen didn't hear this conversation because of his interest in all the football games that were playing on TV.

Marion glanced over to where Stephen was sitting and said, "I guess I'll have to tell Stephen why his uncle is so upset. After all, he wasn't even born when all this happened. We never talked about it at all. All Stephen knows is that you left for New York and your father was very unhappy. I never brought your name up, and if it did come up I never agreed with some of your dad's comments. I'll talk to him tomorrow and try to smooth things over. Meanwhile, let's try and enjoy what's left of the day."

When Benjamin left, he headed to his apartment over the store on Bull Street.

"If he thinks I'll be roped into another deal like the last one, he has another think coming." He found himself mumbling all the way home. All the while Tom tried to explain just how he came by the sword, Benjamin heard only the words "Charlie Pickett" and "tracing providence." Memories of Art Larson's words trying to explain his "honest mistake" about the Davis diary echoed loudly while Tom spoke. He had to leave because he didn't know what he would have done. By the time he reached home he was out of breath; he had to sit a long while in his easy chair to gain his composure. After about an hour, he took out the album he had been looking at ever since Marion mentioned the invitation about dinner. "And to think Elizabeth had something to do with..." He started to cry and slammed the book shut, throwing it across the room.

Tom stopped at the Six Pence. He didn't feel like going home just then. He sat at the bar and ordered a drink. He glanced around at some of the patrons who were laughing, and started to think.

I guess I blew any chance of being a welcomed guest to any of the Adams' family. I never would have said anything if I hadn't seen the way he reacted to Elizabeth in church this morning. I guess I was wrong about that. He sat staring into his drink, oblivious to the laughter of the patrons conversing with each other at the bar. After paying for his drink, he decided to call it a night and headed home.

Chapter 23

Marion arrived at the store shortly after ten the morning after Thanksgiving, and was surprised to find the door locked. Usually, she could smell the aroma of fresh coffee as she entered the shop. Today was different and this concerned her. After opening the door she went to the back stairway and called up.

"Uncle Benjamin, are you up there? Are you alright?" He poked his head around the landing of the stairs and reassured her he was fine and he would be down in a few minutes. She then went into the small kitchen and put on the coffee. It wasn't long before he appeared.

"Good morning; sorry about not having the coffee on." He watched her as she reached for two cups and started to pour.

"Not a problem." She wanted to say something about yesterday, but when she looked at him she just couldn't find the right words. "That's a first for you. I can't remember when I didn't catch the smell of coffee coming through the front door."

"About yesterday," he stammered. "I'm sorry for the way I left your house, but when Tom started in and he mentioned Charlie Pickett and 'finding providence,' it was like waving a red flag in front of a bull. Too many memories surfaced from long ago, and to tell you the truth I really didn't catch much of anything else he said. It was no excuse though for me to upset you and Stephen." Marion noticed the exclusion of Elizabeth's name.

"I understand. I know how difficult it is when certain memories surface. After Dan died suddenly, I remember how the littlest things used to send me into a depression for days. But if you had only heard him out you would have realized he is nothing like his father." Marion explained exactly what Tom intended to do with the sword.

"I'll be a son of a gun. He must think I'm some kind of a nutcase. And Elizabeth…after that wonderful sense of peace that came over me in church. I felt so happy being able to connect to her again, and then hearing, or rather not hearing, what was actually being said and behaving in such a stupid manner."

"Elizabeth understood; she told me as much. Tom, however, left soon after, thinking you would never forget what happened between his father and you."

"I'll have to give them both a call and apologize." Marion went on to tell him what the sword looked like and how it was inscribed, In Honour of Lafayette. "It's too bad it didn't come on the market honestly. Do you think that is the rumor that caused Elizabeth to come home?"

"I think so, and besides, when Stephen went out to the Butlers the other day and found out about the break-in out at the property owned by the Georgia Port Authority. I don't know if you heard Stephen tell that story yesterday."

"Yes, I remember something about them putting up a fence or something like that."

"Well, when Elizabeth and Tom started a search looking to see where his father kept any information concerning his dealings with Pickett, they came upon newspaper clippings about the break-in. Tom said his father used to keep clippings of ads but this was highly unusual, so they started to put two and two together. When Stephen added concrete information about the break-ins, this confirmed that Pickett must have stolen it from the Port."

"I'd like to see that son of a bi…" he stopped mid sentence, "that thief put behind bars. All he has ever done is give antique dealers a bad name."

"Well here's your opportunity. Tom wants to enlist your help to put an end to his thievery. Pickett threatens to drag the Larson name through the mud if Tom doesn't give him a substantial amount of money. He feels that if you and he confront Pickett it will give Tom the upper hand."

"You know, with all this talk about the sword and Revolutionary…it seems I've seen something not too long ago that ties in. Oh well, it's probably the business we're in. Some antiques that we come across have a way of making lasting impressions. Sure, I'll be only too glad to help Tom lasso in that so and so."

Chapter 24

Marion arrived home Friday night to find Stephen packing. He was going to catch an early flight in the morning.

"Did Uncle Benjamin say why he left like he did?" Stephen said as he shoved clothes into a back pack. "He certainly looked mad as hell when he left."

"Yes he did, and he felt very sorry after I explained to him what Tom intends to do about his mess."

"It sure is. I feel sorry for him. I suppose his father figured he would never get caught. Goes to show you. You never know when your number is up." He finished his packing and grinned. When he turned to face his mother, she frowned. She couldn't smile at his last remark.

"Never mind forecasting; is everything in that thing you call a suitcase? It never surprises me how much you guys squeeze into such a small thing."

"Yep, got everything, and I also started dinner. Well sort of, it's all leftovers from yesterday. I made up two plates. All we have to do is heat them in the microwave."

"Good, I'm tired. It was a long day. We spent most of it cataloging a shipment of old books from Tennessee." Just then the phone rang. "I'll get that; you start dinner." She smiled.

"Hi, it's Elizabeth. Just wanted you to know my father called and apologized about yesterday. He also called Tom and did the same. I can't tell you how grateful I am to you for all your help. Tom told him he could take a look at the sword before he returned it, and my father was delighted. He is coming over tonight about eight. I don't know if Stephen would like to see it too, but if he is interested he is welcome."

"I'm glad everything worked out. I'll ask Stephen if he would like to. We were just going to have dinner."

"Great, maybe I'll see you later then. Goodbye." Marion placed the phone in its receiver and walked into the kitchen.

"That was your Aunt Elizabeth. Everything is A-ok between her and Uncle Benjamin. In fact, Tom invited him over to his house tonight to take a look at the discovery. You're invited too if you're interested."

"Maybe I will. Never saw anything like that before. I'm curious." He took his mother's dinner plate out of the microwave and, with a waiter-like gesture, placed it in front of her.

Benjamin walked over to Art Larson's house. *Never thought I would set foot in this house*, he thought as he rang the doorbell. Elizabeth answered and hugged her dad.

"Come in. Tom was just getting some logs; here, let me take your jacket."

"Thanks, but I'll think I'll keep it on until the fire gets started." He walked into the living room and watched as Tom poked at logs in the fireplace.

"Can I get you a drink?" Tom asked as he headed for the wet bar.

"Sure, maybe it will take the chill out of these old bones. Scotch straight up if you have it." Tom fixed the drink and handed it to him while Benjamin settled in a chair near the fire. "I don't know what came over me yesterday." Tom interrupted.

"Forget it; I have. More important is how to nail Charlie Pickett once and for all. I didn't want to call him until I had some kind of a plan in mind. Speaking of which, let me get the sword. Wait till you see it. It's magnificent."

Elizabeth sat next to her father. By this time the fire was blazing. Tom handed the leather case to Benjamin. He put his drink down and took the artifact in his hand. Slowly he patted down the leather case and his fingers followed the embossed letter carving; he then removed the sword from the case. Elizabeth and Tom watched him as his fingers traced over the gold handle and intricately carved mottoes, coats of arms, and engraved scenes from four of the battles in which Lafayette had participated in America. On one side of the blade, an engraving showed a young warrior, Lafayette, dealing a death blow to the British lion; on the other, America, released from her chains, hands the young warrior an olive branch.

"This is magnificent; what detail, what workmanship." He then looked at the leather case and turned it over. After a while, he seemed to show more interest in the leather case than he did in the sword itself. "This case...this case, this engraving. It seems I've seen this before, but I can't place it." He then went back to examining the sword again. Just then the door bell rang. Tom answered the door; it was Stephen and Marion.

"Couldn't miss this opportunity to share in a history-making event." Stephen laughed. Marion sat down while Stephen walked over to his uncle's chair. "This sure is a neat sword. How in the world did these guys ever duel with something this heavy?"

"I don't think they did too much dueling, Stephen," Tom interrupted. "It was more for show than anything else. It's what you would call an ornamental sword."

"Oh, I see, and the case." Stephen looked at the worn leather case. "This embossed lettering. I've seen something like this before...out at the Butler ranch. In fact, the day before Thanksgiving when I went out there to ride, I saw an old saddle with a similar design, in their barn. He buys them at auctions. At dinner that night he told me that some of them were engraved by blacksmiths in the eighteenth century."

"That's it." Benjamin jumped out of his chair, almost spilling the drink in his hand. "That's where I read it. I didn't see it, I read it." All eyes turned to him.

"What are you talking about?" Marion asked, puzzled by his outburst. All eyes were still riveted on him.

"A few weeks ago there was a shipment of rare books from Tennessee. Remember, Marion, we were finishing up today cataloguing them. Well I happened to glance at one and the writing talked about Lafayette and the writer's father. Anyway, the initial on the leather-bound book resembled this design somewhat."

"Could be a clue," said Elizabeth. "Maybe there is another rare find. This one, an honest one." Benjamin, still standing, said he had to leave.

"I want to look for that book right now. There were quite a few so it will take a while." Marion didn't volunteer to start the search. Stephen looked at his watch and said he had better get going as well since he had an early flight. "That's alright, Marion, you can help after you take Stephen to the airport tomorrow." Smiles abounded as everyone said their goodbyes. The night ended on a much happier note than the night before.

Chapter 25

George Bell had spent Thanksgiving with his daughter, Sarah, and her husband. For the first time in many years he had wished she was on one of her shopping sprees with her husband. After he came back from Savannah, he found himself thinking about Kathleen and the pleasant walks in Forsyth Park with the dogs. It wasn't long before the opportunity for a phone call to her presented itself.

"George, did you happen to see the headlines in the *Atlanta Journal* this morning?"

George recognized the voice on the end of the phone. It was Vincent McGuire of Southwest Realty. "Revolutionary Artifact Found in Mulberry Grove; there was something to that rumor after all. You'll have to go back to Savannah and find out more details. The article said an antique dealer contacted the Georgia Port Authority because he was offered a sword presumably owned by Lafayette. The dealer knew the person who presented the artifact to him didn't come by it honestly."

"I'll be a son of a gun. When did all this happen?"

"A few days after Thanksgiving, but the news media didn't get hold of it till now. I'm sure owners of large tracts of land may just be interested in selling off. What do you think?" Normally George didn't respond to Vincent's quick rush to judgment, but he chimed in that yes, he believed there would be. "I'm thinking of opening up a small office somewhere in the Savannah historic district and I'd like you to manage it. What say?"

"Sounds like a great idea. Maybe I can hook my old client into looking at some other properties in the area. When would you like me to go?"

"Soon as possible."

"I'll make a few calls and get the ball rolling, Vince." *What a lucky break*, he thought to himself.

The phone rang and rang. Finally voice mail kicked in. "Welcome to Le Provence…" the message identified no one available so George left word for Kathleen to get in touch with him. He explained that business would take him back and yes he would like to attend her grand opening.

That afternoon when Kathleen checked her voice mail she was ecstatic. "This is wonderful." She too had been thinking about him since he departed Savannah. She realized at Thanksgiving when her boys had come home that they were all grown up. They spent Thanksgiving Day together but as evening approached the two boys wanted to go out on their own, sans mother. Savannah was something new for them to explore so Kathleen encouraged them and named some of the few clubs and places SCAD students frequented. The inn had been completed down to the last detail by the holiday. The boys told her she had done a wonderful job and were happy for her. Somehow she thought they would want to spend more time with her and felt disappointed. George's phone call wiped out any feelings of depression about the Thanksgiving holiday. "This is great; not only will the boys be home but they'll get a chance to meet George."

"Hello, George, this is Kathleen. I got your message. It will be great seeing you again. The opening will be on the 22nd of December. The only thing is Lady…"

"I was hoping you could find me an apartment. It seems I will be in Savannah a while. I suppose you've seen the local papers about the find out at Mulberry."

"Yes, that was something. Did you know the local antique dealer was Tom Larson?"

"I didn't see the article but my realtor told me it was an antique dealer."

"Yes and Elizabeth Adams, you remember her, we met her in the park one day while walking the dogs. Well, she went back to New York. It seems NBC sent her down here because of that rumor and she left with the story. It seems she and Tom were an item a long time ago."

"Is that so? What a coincidence. Anyway, back to what I mentioned about an apartment. Can you help me out?"

"I'll call a realtor today and find out. I'm sure there's something available. You'll have to pay for Lady. Usually the owners require some kind of pet deposit. Will that be a problem?"

"No, not at all. Just let me know so I can start packing. I'm looking forward to seeing you."

"Me too. I certainly enjoy your company. By for now." Kathleen hung the phone up and smiled.

Chapter 26

It hadn't taken Benjamin long to locate the diary after leaving the Larson house. He checked the catalogue file and went right to the shelf where the 1800 rare books were stacked. Carefully, he fingered the leather-worn initialed book and tried to locate the page he had read. Snippets of Stephen's conversation that night about saddles out at the Butler ranch having almost the identical emblem on the sword's case played in his mind. "Where oh where is the page?" He finally found it. "Let me see." He began to read aloud. He then proceeded to turn the pages and little by little it became clear to him the entries were made by a young girl. This young girl was tutored by Eli Whitney. "Wait a minute." He found himself talking out loud to himself. "That piece in the *Savannah Morning News* that I read and Tom found in his father's desk drawer. Could it be this sword of Lafayette became the property of a blacksmith who lived out at the old Nathaniel Greene plantation? But just how did this all happen?" By this time it was three o'clock in the morning and he was exhausted. He put out the lights downstairs in the store and went upstairs to his apartment.

When Marion arrived at the store the next morning, she could smell the aroma of coffee. "Good, that's just what I need. Uncle Benjamin," she called out.

"Back here." His voice came from the kitchen. "Did Stephen get off okay?"

"Yes, we hit some traffic on I95 that tied us up a bit. When we reached the airport, there was a long line, but Stephen had his boarding pass so he went right to the gate. I'm glad the coffee is made."

"Look at some of these entries." Benjamin had placed book marks in the journal that reflected ties to the sword. After reading the entries Marion remarked.

"That young girl must have been one of Nathaniel Greene's daughters. When she grew up and got married she probably moved to Tennessee. It's easy enough to find out. I'll check it out at the library. This is great. This book may well establish the providence Tom needs. The Port Authority will be glad to get it back; why don't we call him and tell him about this journal? If he asks you to confront Charlie Pickett, will you do it.?"

"We'll see, but I would really like to see Pickett in jail for all the rotten deals he has gotten away with for so long."

"The good thing that comes out of all this is we have a rare find, only we came by it honestly. Wonder what it will go for? Any ideas?"

"The Port Authority may make an offer because it establishes a relationship between the blacksmith with Lafayette, and possibly want it in the restoration plans of the plantation. Meanwhile I'll call around some auction houses to see and get a ball park figure to work with in the event they do."

"I'll stop by the library and look up a biography on Nathaniel Greene. I'm sure it will shed more light on this. Let's give Tom a call. Do you want to or shall I?"

"I will because I'd like to know what he intends to do about Pickett."

"Ok, then after I finish my coffee, I'll head out to the library." Marion finished her coffee, rinsed the cup and placed it on the drain board and left.

"Hello, Tom, Benjamin Adams here. I found that journal where I found out some information about the sword. If you'd like, I'll bring it over so you can see it."

"That's great news, Benjamin; I'm still at my dad's house finishing up some minor details. Now would be a good a time as ever. But you probably don't want to close up shop."

"I could come over between twelve and one. We usually close an hour for lunch. Is that alright?"

"Sure, thanks again; this will give me some leverage with Charlie Picket. I can't wait to nail that bas…so and so."

"My thoughts exactly, Tom; see you at noon."

Chapter 27

After Tom read the excerpts from the diary that Benjamin brought over, he told him what Charlie Pickett had threatened to do. "Sounds just like him," said Benjamin. "If he is threatened with a jail sentence he doesn't care who he takes down with him, even if it isn't true." Elizabeth, who was sitting next to Tom, cast her eyes downward. Benjamin hadn't expected her to be there at this meeting. He got up from his chair and started pacing back and forth. "I'd like to see that so and so go to jail. That's the right place for that thief." Elizabeth, who by now had gone into the kitchen because she didn't want to interfere, knew she would start to cry if her father insisted that Tom name Pickett as the culprit. She loved Tom and hoped her father would listen to the plan he had.

"You're right, Benjamin, but the way things are now between Elizabeth and me, if you insist on not listening to what I intend to do, I don't feel it would be right for me to ask her to marry me." Benjamin sat down on the chair and picked up the diary.

"What do you intend to do?" he said, smoothing his hand over the book.

"I was going to call and tell him I had told you about it and that I intend to give it back to the Port. In exchange I won't tell the Port who it was that gave it to me. In this way he avoids jail but my name won't be dragged through the mud."

"What makes you think that would work? He could very well say that I would give him up because he knows how I despise what he stands for." Benjamin got up from the chair and waved the diary in his hand. "You know, as much as I'd like to see that bastard in jail I think I will be satisfied because of this find I came by honestly. I'll go along with your plan, but I think you should leave out the part about telling me. If he thinks it's just between you two, he may just opt for it."

"Thanks, Benjamin." Elizabeth, who overheard the conversation, came back into the room and put her arms around her father.

"Thanks, Dad. I know how you have been hurt by all of this. Now Tom and I can make it official about our wedding plans. As soon as I get back from New York and hand in the story, we intend to set a date. We just wanted to have all this behind us before we did, and you made it possible. You have made us so very happy!"

"I'm happy for you both," Benjamin said as he put the book down and shook Tom's hand. "I had better get back to the store. Marion went to the library to check on some background information on the diary."

"The diary, the Port may want as well," Tom said.

"Well they can have it," Benjamin laughed, "but at a nice price; after all, I can establish providence."

When Benjamin returned to the store, Marion was back from the library.

"I was right about Nathaniel Greene having daughters. This diary must have belonged to Cornelia Greene. She was the oldest daughter and when she married she moved to Tennessee."

"That establishes a friendship between the blacksmith and Lafayette, but how the sword landed in Mulberry Grove may always remain a mystery."

"You're probably right, but the Port Authority will hold claim to it because of the circumstances surrounding the find. I'm sure they will appreciate the fact that Tom is an honest and reputable dealer. I just hope the Port is satisfied with him returning it and not giving up Pickett's name."

"I think it will work out. I'm only sorry that Pickett doesn't go to jail, but at least he can't depend on a place where to peddle his stolen property. Now that Tom and Elizabeth are planning a wedding, I wouldn't want to throw a wrench in their happiness. I'll just have to 'move on' as they say."

"A wedding. I'm so happy for them both. Did they say anything about a date?"

"No, Elizabeth has to go back to New York and turn in her story. I suppose she will be back at Christmas."

"That's wonderful. I got a letter from Colleen and she has her flight booked for the 22nd. Our family will all be together for Christmas. I can't wait. Oh by the way, I thought you would like to read this biography on Nathaniel Greene so I checked it out of the library. It sheds some light on the background of Cornelia's entries in her diary."

"Thanks, think I will. Meanwhile I'll call around to see just how much our find will bring at auction."

Chapter 28

NBC had been more than pleased with Elizabeth's story about the artifact. She emphasized the fact about the antique dealer having such wonderful ethics, that when it was offered to him to sell on the black market he declined. What she failed to do was tell about her past relationship with Tom twenty years ago. Because of her accomplishment, her employer agreed to give her some time at Christmas to return to her family in Savannah. There were only a few of her colleagues that knew the entire story, but somehow news got back to the powers that be about her upcoming wedding and NBC thought that down the road there could be another feature story about an NBC anchor woman who finds romance investigating antiques in her home town. Elizabeth said she would have to check with her fiancé about that first.

"Tom, I have reservations on Continental Airlines out of Newark on the 22nd of December. I should arrive at noon or a little after. My boss loved the story and he was so impressed that when he found out I was getting married he wants to incorporate my uncovering the sword into another feature story. I'll discuss it with you later. I miss you and can't wait to see you. Have you put your father's house on the market yet?"

"No, I want to think about that a bit. I'm looking forward to seeing you too. How long will you be able to stay?"

"My boss is giving me three weeks. Maybe after Christmas we can take a short cruise to the Bahamas. The weather up here has been awfully cold. Have you seen Marion or Dad lately?"

"No, I've been pretty busy finishing up the business at the store. I never realized how much detail work there is in this business. My dad took care of most of it and there was a lot of catching up to do after the Pickett deal. I'm glad your father made a nice profit on the Greene diary. It kind of makes up for the raw deal he got on the Davis deal."

"Yes, he told me about it when I called him the other day. I also spoke to Marion and she told me Colleen was flying in from Paris on the 22nd. She will be arriving in Newark the morning of the 22nd so maybe I'll be on the same flight when she changes planes. Continental has a direct flight out of Newark and that's her carrier out of Paris."

"We have a lot to talk about, honey, when you get down here. Can't wait to see you. Love you."

"Me too; see you soon." Elizabeth hung the phone up and stared out the window at the falling snow. "The Bahamas sounds like a great place."

The morning of the 22nd Marion ran some errands for wrapping paper. She wanted the tree and all the gifts finished and done when the children arrived. Stephen wouldn't be getting in until the 23rd because of some make-up exams and she knew once Colleen arrived there would be no time for last minute things. "There," she said as she stood back from the tree to admire her handy work, "everything is done." All the gifts were wrapped and placed at the bottom of the tree. The Crib was centered as a focal point. She fingered the statues and the babe and silently prayed that everyone would arrive safely for the holiday. "Look at the time," she glanced at her watch, "I'd better get going."

At the airport Christmas music was playing and it lent an air to the holiday spirit as commuters hugged and kissed upon arrivals and departures. Marion looked up at the arrival and departure schedule. *Good, the flight from Newark is on time. I wonder if Elizabeth caught the same flight out as Colleen,* she thought.

Just then she spied Tom coming out of Starbucks. "Tom, over here," she called. Tom looked around at the sound of his name and waved to Marion.

"I see you've got the holiday spirit," he said, pointing to her lapel decoration of Santa on her jacket.

"I can't wait to see my Colleen. I've missed her so much. You know Elizabeth and she may be on the same flight. Colleen's flight was to get in at six at Newark and she was scheduled for the same flight to Savannah as Elizabeth."

"That would be nice. I'm sure Elizabeth could pick her out of the crowd."

"She should. Colleen looks just like her. I showed her a picture of her when we had lunch at the Six Pence." They walked over to a table nearby and sat down, observing the commuters. The announcement of the Newark flight at gate 2 came over the loudspeaker and they both headed over to the arrival area. It wasn't long before both Elizabeth and Colleen came up the ramp, busily chatting away. Marion called out and caught her daughter's eye. Colleen broke away from Elizabeth's side and ran the rest of the way to her mother.

"Mom, Mom, it's so good to see you!" They hugged and kissed each other.

Tom rushed to greet Elizabeth and swept her up in his arms, and they too embraced passionately. When the greeting was over the group began exchanging conversations, but because everyone was talking at once no one could make out just what was being said.

At the luggage carousel, the group split. Colleen and her mother said their goodbyes to Tom and Elizabeth. "Mom, Aunt Elizabeth told me all about her visit and the artifact. I can't believe it. Wait until you hear what I have to add about Lafayette!